Mr. Kitty Wanders Ireland

Tim Cross

AOS Publishing, 2025
Copyright © 2025 Tim Cross

All rights reserved under International
and Pan-American copyright conventions

ISBN: 978-1-998662-73-9

Cover Design: Meredith Lindsay

Visit AOS Publishing's website:
www.aospublishing.com

Prologue

Mr. Kitties' adventures bring him to a spirit circle of supernatural beings formed with hope for the future. The story evolves around finding and saving Runda, a leprechaun who protects the secret spirit stone that defines the birth and death of a universe.

The spirit circle works together to save the universe from the tyrannical Balor, who uses his evil eye to turn his perceived enemies to stone with his powerful stare.

Balor will stop at nothing to gain the power of the spirit stone. Mr. Kitty has come to Ireland to learn but has become entangled in a story beyond his control. He gives of himself as his peaceful journey becomes a dangerous mission.

Experience a dimensional travelling cat, building friendships in a world steeped in Irish tales. Mr. Kitty, by a stroke of chance, becomes a key player in the unfolding events, ultimately becoming immortalized in its history.

Mr. Kitty meets Irish Giants and Goddesses while learning more about the characters' backgrounds. From Finn McCool to Dagda and Danu; a story evolves into the tragedy and resilience of the Spirit.

Life is only a moment to wait for forever.

Pick up your spirit from the mud that binds your feet.

Set sights on your star to share its guiding light.

Give up the fight and begin small steps toward the goal.

Hindsight is the best insight to foresight.

Learn from the struggle; it builds strength and character.

Knowledge is knowing that the end is the beginning.

Table of Contents

Ireland

Ireland
Tory Island
Dunluce Castle
Randalstown
Slingo
Uisneach Hilll
Cong
Cliffs of Moher
Grange Stone Circle
Killarney
Ring of Kerry
Rathlin Island
Giants Gateway
Lough Neagh
Ballynoe Stone Circle
Newgrange
Dublin
Old Head
Drombeg Stone Circle

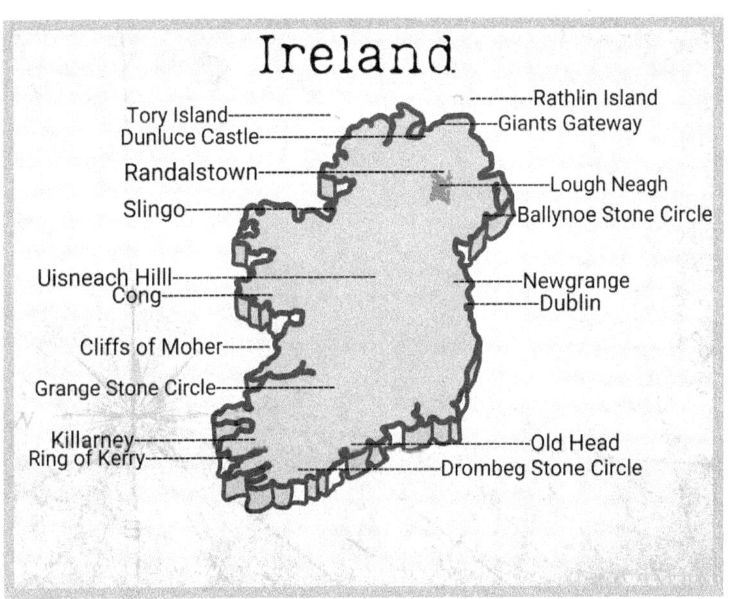

Spirit Circle

Chapter 1 Tir na nOg

To dream is to live life to its fullest.
Start a journey with the most enduring challenges
to impact your outcome.
Taking the chance
It is a potential worth exploring.
In the end, you will only give yourself
credit for efforts made.
Respect for yourself is required, as is a willingness to change.
The journey is a staircase where the answers are questions,
when you set forth a beginning.

Mr. Kitty, a precarious cat, held on to his dream of travelling to Ireland. Drawn to the culture, music, and castles, he couldn't wait to visit the tragic love that endured through the ages, echoing pride and longing to feel the peace and love.

Ireland's history is like no other, and he could feel it approaching as he flew over the land heading to Dublin. His first impression of September's beautiful, lush landscape was heart-lightening, with the rocky shores blending into gorgeous, rolling green hills.

Mr. Kitty stood on the seat with his paws against the window as he saw Dublin approaching. The plane was bouncing as turbulence pushed it around. This caused Mr. Kitty to feel nervous enough to sit back down and dig his claws into the seat.

The airport was no less turbulent, as people rushed around in every direction. No one looked down to see him as they all dogged each other, pulling their suitcases, nearly running over Mr. Kitty a few times.

He showed his true cat skills as he saw an exit and stealthily navigated his way out the door. Bouncing through the streets, he is filled with joy as he makes his way here. Having no worries in the world, he opened his heart and mind to a new perspective on life.

The buildings of thirteenth-century architecture defined Dublin's magnificence. Mr. Kitty wandered the streets and felt amazed with each corner he turned. He met people who were more than eager to spend time with him and share their food and drink with him. His first night was spent down by the river that ran through the city.

Mr. Kitty curled up under a bridge, at peace with a full belly, listening to the sound of the night. The swans moving through the water and the city's sound blend to a balance of nature. As he walked through the woods, Mr. Kitty drifted into a slumber filled with dreams of fairies and flower petals.

His first day in Ireland was fantastic. The air was still, and the skies were clear. Being an early riser, he was eager to begin the adventure. Mr. Kitty walked through the quiet streets in the early morning as the sun showed pillars of light between the buildings. He discovered a small café by the river and had a delicious breakfast.

Feeling at home in Dublin and greeted with smiles, he loved the light-hearted mood that set the tone for good times.

"Hello kitty," a little girl called from a bench in a park. She looked like an angel to Mr. Kitty. Sitting in a long dress of pale green and beige with scattered sparkles caught by the sun. Her soft red hair brushed over her pale skin. Her pretty green eyes pulled him in.

Mr. Kitty, intrigued, silently strolled over to brush up against her leg. "Oh, how handsome you are," she said. "What's your name, little guy?"

Mr. Kitty was too shy to let her know he could understand English and had his own way of speaking the language.

"Where are you wandering off to on this beautiful day?" She asked.

"I'm not sure where I'm going. But you can call me Kitty," Mr. Kitty said in a soft voice. The girl was sure she understood what he was saying. Shocked, she replied, "Did you say your name is Kitty?"

"Yes, what's your name?" Mr. Kitty answered, looking up at the girl.

"I am Clio." She said with a smile. Then she jumped down to pet him closer.

"Do you know which way is north?" Mr. Kitty asked. Clio was so excited that she let out a giggle.

"I just love meeting interesting strangers, especially a talking cat," Clio said, leaning down to hug him. "Yes, north is that way," she said, pointing.

"Where would you like to go?" Clio asked, hoping he would say with her.

"I am going to the Giant's Causeway in Northern Ireland," Mr Kitty answered, not knowing the journey ahead or how far it would be.

"That is a beautiful spot, full of wonder, but that is a long way on foot," Clio said, concerned.

"I am ready for the challenge." Mr. Kitty said, looking north, thinking that maybe it would be better to stay here and make a new friend in Clio. He stood up and started to walk.

"Be sure to check out Newgrange along the way, it has a kinda energy," Clio said with a smile, as she ran to meet up with her mother. "Bye, Kitty." She said, looking back as she ran.

"What did she mean by a kinda energy?" Mr. Kitty thought to himself. He was joyful and ignited in his heart to finally discover Ireland. Heading north to travel counterclockwise around the island, Mr. Kitty was still determined to discover the adventure ahead with his minimal journey plan before his tiny feet.

Growing exhausted as he walked steadily, the midday sun became hot, and his thirst turned his mouth to sandpaper as he trudged along. His belly rumbled as he became weary of the decision to take on Ireland as his next adventure.

Like a mirage off in the distance, a river seemed to get further away as he walked closer. His feet dragged, growing heavier as the dust covered his little white paws. Mr. Kitty was so hot and thirsty as he made it to the river and threw himself in with a flop. He was delighted to find fresh water in the Boyne River.

Finding new life, the cool water sent a shock through his veins and lit a spark in his heart, reminding him of his love of adventure. He floated on his back, taking in the beauty as the river pushed him under a great oak tree, which brought back memories of the big oak on the hill next to his home, where his friends Wisdom the Owl and Dally Dear lived.

Mr. Kitty came out of the Boyne to take refuge in the shade under the great oak of Ireland. Sitting in peace, leaning against the thick trunk, he fell into a slumber. He was drifting into shallow dreams, where he wasn't sure if he was awake or dreaming. A druid glided out of the shadows from behind the oak as he sang:

Early in the east, as the sun warms my soul.
It takes away the pain of the long, fantastic night.
The moon sends her love as she fades to the west.
Great oak is my pillar, as I share my guiding light.
In dark realms, I will roam till the earth grounds me home.
Cool water at my roots fills the knowledge of my dreams
'Till I joyfully head west with the sky as my ceiling.

He stopped suddenly when Mr. Kitty jumped to his feet, feeling honoured to be in the presence of such a guru. He was a tall, rugged man with a calm, dignified presence and a wealth of untold wisdom. His long hair hugged his face, casting a shadow over the weathered wrinkles.

"Well, hello, little kitty. I'm Dair," he said, pulling back the cloak that covered his face. "What brings a kitty to the foot of this oak, blessing my presence?"

Mr. Kitty knew the mystery and greatness of the man standing before him, stumbling nervously. "I'm Kit Cat, but you can call me Kitty."

"Well, nice to meet you, Kitty; What may I do for you on this fine afternoon?"

"I seek shade from the sun, a cool drink, and my belly could use a snack," said Mr. Kitty, as a low rumble echoed in his stomach. Feeling embarrassed, he hung his head.

"Well, the River Boyne just happens to have fresh water to quench your thirst; a delicious salmon will fill the belly, and the leaves upon my tree will shade the sun for as long as you desire," said Dair, crouching down to reassure his new friend.

"You are very generous, good sir. It has been a very long morning to get here. My feet are getting ahead of me, and I need a rest." Mr. Kitty had to lie down; the day's weight could no longer be held.

"Lighten the load, young kitty, and I will prepare a lunch for you."

Dair entered the water's edge and placed his hands in the calmly flowing river. He quickly pulled out a large salmon. He took it to the grass and held it down as he whispered something to himself, and the salmon gave up the struggle. Dair then continued to prepare lunch for Mr. Kitty while he rested his tired, dusty paws.

"*Ta dinnear a seirbheail,* little kitty," said Dair while Mr. Kitty slowly rose. The salmon Dair had prepared smelled better than anything Mr. Kitty had ever smelled. Dair had cooked the fish over a small fire he had built while Mr. Kitty rested his eyes.

Mr. Kitty dove into the salmon, hungry from his long journey. The salmon was mouth-watering and delicious as he took more bites. Mr. Kitty was filled with salmon, while Dair ate no fish. He sat staring at the trees on the other side of the river.

"Dair, will you not have a taste of salmon and join me for dinner?"

A slight smile on the corner of Dair's mouth seemed to glow as he said, "No, Kitty, I've had my nourishment this morning."

Mr. Kitty thought about how he could not want any of this delicious salmon. It warmed him up and gave him tingling from the top of his head to the tip of his paws. He felt an intense sense of bliss upon meeting Dair. He became flooded with emotions and needed to ask Dair a few questions before continuing his journey.

"Kitty, is there something you wish to ask me?"

"How did you know?"

"I see the look of question on your face. I've learned to read people over time. Please feel free to ask anything."

"What is your biggest inspiration in seeking wisdom?"

"That is a big question for such a little guy. I like to read and live the story. It's no different than you being here. You are living in the adventure you seek. Wisdom will present itself from moment to moment," said Dair

"Second, are Leprechauns and fairies real? I have heard stories and come to Ireland hoping to see them," Mr. Kitty said.

Dair laughed with a full-on belly laugh at this question. "Well, Kitty, I have yet to see one here, but both are as real as your imagination is true. There is no doubt in my mind that there are many mysteries of this world yet to be discovered. The spirit is alive in Ireland, and with curiosity, patience, and love in your heart, you may find what you are searching for."

"Thanks, Dair. I will take this as a positive and keep my eyes open. I do have another question."

"Please, Kitty?"

"I am new to Ireland and unsure what I should do next. My adventure is just exploring places, meeting people, and learning as much as possible here," said Mr. Kitty.

"Ireland has a lot to teach; your adventures could take you anywhere on the island, and there is knowledge to gain from the friends you meet. You're heading north, and I dare not sway you from your chosen path.

"To answer your question, I will respond with a question. Where would you like to go?"

"Well, there is much I would like to see, and I don't have as much time as needed to see it all," said Mr. Kitty.

"I would love to help you on your journey. I am a spiritual druid with skills unlike any you will likely meet here. I will help you travel long distances in a short time, though I will not stay with you all the time; there is always help needed in my line of work," said Dair.

"Dair, there are several places I would like to visit. I am headed north to see the Giant's Causeway. I hope to see a few castles and other mysterious ruins along the way. Finally, I have dreamt of visiting the cliffs of Mohr," said Mr. Kitty.

"One step at a time, Kitty. Come with me, then; I will help you on your way."

Dair led Mr. Kitty into a hole that had naturally formed in the back of the giant oak tree, and they disappeared as they walked in.

Chapter 2 Newgrange

Joining in oneness finds the support necessary for the story to
unfold.
The thinness of time needs family and friends as glue for the
journey to exist.
Support in the circle will build a structure strong enough to
endure its limitations.
Reach out into imagination till the darkness becomes light.
When you don't see the light, you are the light.
The light guides the trail that is sought;
A stone in the wind dives deep into the mystery of the past.
Illuminate West brings meaning to empathy and respect for the
dead,
those who light the pathway home.

The wind whistled in Mr. Kitty's ears as Dair took him into a doorway at the base of the great oak tree. Opening up Mr. Kitty's sense of wonder, as any tired sore muscles he had faded like a passing dream. The world on the other side of the passage seemed bright and timeless, as if his weary body had just woken.

The birds chirped, and the river trickled as they entered a world very similar to the one where Mr. Kitty was from. Although he felt calm and had no need to hurry through his journey to see everything in Ireland, he realized he was already a part of Ireland.

"Dair, what just happened? We walked into a hole in the great oak, which seemed to be a passage to another world." Asked Mr. Kitty in amazement.

"We have entered the extended reality of your existence; you have been here before, Kitty, though you may not recall. The way I see it, your world is my dream world. I have learned and evolved between this world and the other," said Dair.

Mr. Kitty knew that Dairs' roots run deep in untold wisdom. He sat and looked up at Dair, wanting to ask more questions.

"How did you take me from your dream world to my dream world?"

"I am a teacher of nature and wisdom of the way of truth, light, and love. It's not a common practice to escort someone from one world to another. You are unique, Kitty. I sense your passion for knowledge and adventure, driven by the purest intentions. Our worlds may be separate, though it is not impossible to navigate between them. Your world is like a mirror image of our world."

As Dair finished his sentence, Mr. Kitty's eyes widened, and he was sure he had seen a fairy sitting on a branch hiding above the passage into the great tree.

Mr. Kitty whispered, "Don't move; I think I see a fairy there." He said, pointing to the tree.

Dair smiled seeing his friend. "Hazel, don't be shy. Come down and meet our new friend, Kit Cat."

"Please! I am of no harm," said Mr. Kitty.

The fairy, with long blond hair and a shimmering aura, floated down in a sparkling green dress to greet Mr. Kitty.

"Please call me Kitty. That's what my friends call me." Mr. Kitty felt so much joy, but had to hold back from showing his excitement at seeing Hazel's wings sparkle in the sunlight.

"Pleasure, Kitty; I'm Hazel. What brings you to the River Boyne?" Landing next to Mr. Kitty, standing as tall as his chin.

"I have come a long way to explore Ireland, to see the beauty, and to experience the island's lore," Mr. Kitty said as he started to understand what Dair meant by living the experience and taking in the moment.

"Welcome to one of the most beautiful places on Earth," said Hazel."The magic of nature I can show you here will be like none other. You made a good decision for your travels," said Hazel.

"I have always wanted to come here. It reminds me of home," said Mr. Kitty

"Where have you come from?" asked Hazel.

"Canada," Mr. Kitty replied.

"Where are your travel mates?" asked Hazel.

"I have come alone this time; I decided to come spontaneously to follow my heart and go where my dreams lead me. I have always wanted to come here," said Mr. Kitty.

"I would love to join you if you are okay with that," said Hazel.

"Yes! Of course," answered Mr. Kitty.

"Follow me, then. If you haven't been here before, I recommend you come with me just over Tara Hill, where you will find something built by the mystics," said Hazel.

"Oh, yes! That's why I am here. I don't know what it is, but I am very interested in learning."

"From what I know, this place is a common area for astral travellers and spirits going west or anywhere in the universe connected to the light grid. It is like a social gathering spot, since many travellers are coming and going. Here in *Tir na nOg,* we refer to this place as *Soilsiu thiar,* or Illuminate West."

The three walked over the hill to see a large gathering of unusual creatures and humans.

"Welcome to what you would refer to as 'Newgrange' in your world," said Dair.

Mr. Kitty was amazed by the number of spirits gathered here.

Dair saw Mr. Kitty's wide eyes as they walked closer.

"In *Tir na nOg,* we have a different form of travel; we can travel on light waves over great distances, and Newgrange tunes spirits into a particular frequency to help them travel," said Dair.

"This place is great; I would never have imagined a place like this could have existed alongside my world. A gathering beyond my dreams," said Mr. Kitty as his tail puffed out, feeling nervous and excited.

"We can join the gathering if you wish. The frequency radiates out from the centre of the Bru. Those who enter have a choice of transport on the frequency radiating out, never to return to this place again. It seems to be a one-way journey. Further out from the centre, it will give a different frequency destined for other locations. The standing stones help guide travellers to where they want to go," said Dair

As they walked closer, the sound of music filled the air. There were plenty of drums, whistles, and stringed instruments. This place is very social, offering food and drinks.

"Now, this is a lively gathering," said Mr. Kitty.

"Yes!" said Hazel. "It's like a community monument, somewhere to meet to share stories, common interests, or friendly arguments."

"During certain times of the year, there are heartbreaking moments to honour and remember those who have travelled west, never to return," said Hazel.

As they entered the crowd, Mr. Kitty noticed dwarfs, giants, fairies, people, warriors, splendid swans, druids, and Elves of various shapes and sizes.

Mr. Kitty was in his glory, walking around the crowd, feeling at home even though he was miles away and not even part of his realm anymore. The sounds of music, talk, and many people having a good time made Mr. Kitty feel welcome in this ancient land.

Then, as the clouds parted, it seemed as though the sky was opening, and Mr. Kitty could see something dark flying through them. He could see the smoke flying toward them, but as it got closer, he panicked and ran around Dair and Hazel.

"A meteor is going to hit us!" Mr. Kitty said. Dair looked up to see Mr. Kitty's concerns.

"Don't worry, Kitty," said Dair.

"How are you not worried about a meteor on the way?" said Mr. Kitty.

"It's not a meteor, but it could still be dangerous. We will have to see what presents," Dair said.

Mr. Kitty watched the object get closer, though no one seemed fazed by it. He continued to watch as it got closer, and then he could see it had wings and was breathing fire.

"I'm sure I am seeing a dragon approaching us," Mr. Kitty said with a rattle in his throat, tucking under Dair's long cloak.

"That's what I was afraid of," said Dair.

"What do you mean?" asked Mr. Kitty.

"He brings word," said Dair.

Mr. Kitty looked up toward Newgrange to see an enormous creature he had never seen before spreading its white wings and landing behind the half-stone circle of Newgrange. It was a three-headed dragon. Mr. Kitty was terrified and in awe, but no one seemed to move; it was as though the dragon was home and hadn't visited in a while. People crowded around to admire him.

"Kitty, that is Dagda." The crowd broke out into song to welcome him.

May the light shine bright,
Midst the darkness of the night,
Forever bathe in love,
Feed the harvest from above.
Innocence is your gift,
Immortality as you lift.
Please be it good tidings for we live in your abidings.

The dragon stood for a moment to listen to the song. He gave a full-throated roar, with three heads lifted to the air, and shot a brilliant light show of white-blue flames, accompanied by a hit of red and orange hues. The crowd cheered as the dragon sank into the ground. The group returned to its previous focus.

"Where did it go, Dair?" asked Mr. Kitty.

"He just arrived; he hasn't gone anywhere. You just may meet him, Kitty. He is the god of wisdom, life, and death," said Hazel.

"He holds all knowledge and shares it all if you have the right questions," said Dair.

"How do we meet this master? I sure would enjoy some time with him," said Mr. Kitty.

"Patience, Kitty; patience is the way to Dagda. He has been around so long that he doesn't rush much. He takes his sweet time to do anything," said Dair.

"I'm sure with all the knowledge of the cosmos, that food, drink, and music are a priority for his homecoming. He must clear his head before making any hasty speeches," said Dair.

"Should we make our way toward Newgrange? I would sure like to look closer," said Kitty, turning to walk through the crowd.

"Just remember, Kitty, this tool Dagda built will tune you into frequencies outside of your mind. So be mindful of where we are, not to get crossed signals or end up somewhere else in the universe," said Dair.

"I didn't realize it was that powerful a construction," said Mr. Kitty.

"Indeed, it is, especially for those most vulnerable, who are open-hearted like yourself. Kitty, you are a rare breed, ready to learn new information, and willing to help without question. You will do well in *Tir na nOg*. But this also leaves you exposed to the elements, and if you don't know how to control your emotions and block negative energy, you could get swept away by the moment or misled by illusions and delusions," said Dair.

The three walked through the field closer to the entrance, hoping to meet Dagda, when Mr. Kitty bumped into an ill-kept elf about two feet tall. Mr. Kitty stood to make eye contact with the dirty elf. Hazel instantly dropped to Mr. Kitty's side to distance him from the elf.

"What have we here?" asked the elf.

"Back off, Glic!" Hazel said.

"Hey now, I'm just wondering who our guest is. I haven't seen you around," said Glic.

"He's a friend of mine and has my blessing to roam our land in peace," said Dair.

"With times the way they are, I just have to watch out for what's happening. Is it a coincidence that Dagda shows up at the same time as a kitty? It makes me wonder," Glic said.

"Nothing to wonder about; a coincidence sometimes is just a coincidence," Dair said.

"Well, Kitty, if you're in Dair's service, whatever you need, I'm at your service. I can be handy in sticky situations," said Glic.

"Thanks, Glic. We won't need your service," said Hazel.

"Just paying my dues; I got my eye on you. I mean, if you need me, I'm around."

The strange little elf disappeared behind a standing stone. Dair looked up and made eye contact with a tall, heavyset man in a badge jacket that reached his knees and a long beard. The crowd parted when he walked. He came directly over to Dair and hugged him as he let out the loudest belly laugh or roar one could let out.

"Dair, my friend, I have missed you while travelling. I trust you are well," said the man.

"Indeed, Dagda. I hope you bring good news," said Dair.

"Aye! Straight to business, is ya? I require your assistance. The spirit stone is missing and should be secured," said Dagda.

At that moment, looking down, Dagda noticed Kitty peeking out from under Dair's cloak.

"Who is this little one? What brings you here?" asked Dagda.

"I'm Kitty, Sir!"

"That you are," said Dagda.

"I have, by chance, come to you," Mr. Kitty said.

"Chance, have you?" Looking at Dair, he said, "Well, your chance of happening may be just the help we need during this time of peril. We must contact my son Finn to find the spirit stone," said Dagda. "Kitty! Meet the dragon," Dair said.

Chapter 3 The Giants' Gateway

Fear is a hurdle that must be overcome.
The emotion felt is not a weakness
but a strength that enlightens your awareness.
The bridge between the walls of your mind
shall not be broken
until you alone illuminate the illusions.
The personal struggle of others is a path to strengthen the
outcome,
both for you, the one you help, and those who live on the web.
Extending a helping hand will vibrate a healthy hope
resonating with peace and love,
two of the most essential constructs that bind the universe.
Connect honour and trust,
and you bridge the gap between misconceptions and delusions.

Mr. Kitty's adventure had led him to a place he would never have dreamed of going. He was standing at the feet of his new friend, Dair, and calming the fairy Hazel. He made it to *Soilsiu thiar*, known as Newgrange, six thousand years ago in the mist world, when the area was very high-frequency and active in the spirit world.

Mr. Kitty was bewildered, looking up at Dagda's incredible spirit. Dagda had just proposed a dangerous mission for Dair, and now Mr. Kitty seemed to be getting involved, regardless of whether he wanted to.

"Dagda, how do you suppose I have anything to contribute to find Finn, whom I don't know, and locate the spirit stone, which I didn't know existed till now?" asked Mr. Kitty.

"Kitty, you have much to offer. Give yourself more credit; it will build your confidence," said Dagda.

"You are not of this plane, so your frequency is contained to yourself, and you are very soft on your feet. With these two qualities, you can be nearly invisible to the senses of potentially harmful spirits in our world. Not to mention, your size is perfect for quickly getting into and out of tight spots. I entrust you with Dair and Hazel; you are ideal for getting the job done and ensuring the safety of the island.

"We are in dire need, as the stone will not only protect our life here in *Tir na nOg*, but in the wrong hands, it will threaten life as you know it in your world. It's potential destruction." Mr. Kitty's eyes widened as Dagda continued, "Some misguided souls believe that our connection with the other world threatens our security and 'pureness'. This bond is symbiotic; we need each other to survive. Theft of the stone can generate a false sense of power, which in the wrong hands can be disastrous," said Dagda.

Mr. Kitty looked around nervously at all his new friends, and Hazel also had a blank look on her face.

"Who wants to save our world?" Dagda asked in a way that made a dangerous mission almost sound like a walk in the park.

Mr. Kitty didn't know what to think about this, but seeing Dagda and Dair, he found a confidence within him that he didn't think he had. "I'm in," Mr. Kitty said bravely.

"I'm in, too. How dare this ignorance get as far as it did?" said Hazel sternly.

"Dark energy is clouded and abundant: if misguided, it can be difficult to recognize until it is too late. It accounts for a significant portion of our potential energy. If used strategically with a heartfelt purpose, it can be a powerful ally to tap into, but on the other side of the coin, if used for the wrong purpose, it can backfire," said Dair.

"Energy needs a recipe," Dagda continued. "With wrong emotions and thoughts, we are all in big trouble."

"I am at your service, Dagda," Dair said, placing a hand on Dagda's shoulder. "What shall we do?"

"Please go see Finn. He is keeping the secret about the one who protects the treasure, and he may be able to lead you to the next clue to help you find the stone," said Dagda.

"Are you coming with us?" asked Mr. Kitty.

"No, Kitty, I am easily recognized and carry a lot of energy. I don't want to jeopardize the mission. I'll remain here at Newgrange to uncover some info and possibly distract the thief from your presence," said Dagda. "You three carry on as if you are sightseeing and unaware that the spirit stone is missing. Ask questions wearily, and do not bring attention to your true mission."

"I can do that-wander around the island unaware of what I am doing or where I am going. Check!" said Mr. Kitty.

"I have not seen Finn in a very long time," said Dair, having grown up like brothers with him. They bonded over a shared love of nature and to protect it from tyrants. Though rough on the outside and passionate on the battlefield, he was a lover at heart, finding the love of his life in a deer. "Where is Finn these days?"

"He has taken refuge on the shore at the Giants' Gateway, which he built to block this world and the other world from Balor, who has been trying to push through," said Dagda. "Finn sits in reflection, blaming himself for many things, including losing his beloved wife."

"We will go see him to lend a shoulder and bear the weight of his burden," said Dair.

"Where are we going?" Mr. Kitty asked, excitedly walking in a circle, brushing Dair and Dagda's ankles.

"We are going to the Giants' Gateway to find Finn McCool," said Hazel.

"It's a sad mission, but I'm pleased to experience the gateway," said Mr. Kitty.

"Live for the moment, Kitty. It's okay to be happy. It will add a diversion layer to our mission. Be curious and ask questions. I hope you find safety in your travels," said Dagda. That stone standing over there will take you to the gateway, " he said, pointing. Remember to be mindful and open your eyes to the light and mist, for they will guide you in darkness."

Just as he finished his words, he was pulled away by a group of admirers. "Dagda! Dagda! Come play us a tune," they asked.

Dair, Hazel, and Mr. Kitty walked toward the large standing stone before Newgrange. As they approached, Mr. Kitty started having flashes of visions of family, friends, and places he had been and wanted to go. He began to feel heavy and sleepy, and was about to pass out by the time they reached the stone.

"Kitty!" Hazel said.

"Only a few more steps; make sure you touch the stone. Focus and stay alert," said Dair.

Mr. Kitty reached the stone with a heavy head full of visions. He curled up and reached his tail to touch the stone; he saw darkness and mist on the water as the moon's light lit the shoreline. He saw the fire burning in the water as a shadow tried to contain the lava and fire. His tail touched the stone with Dair and Hazel.

Mr. Kitty whipped through the mist of colour and was quickly transported. He opened his eyes and sat on the shoreline next to what looked like a giant rock camel as the waves crashed. It was evening, and the setting sun lit up the sky, giving the mist on the water a tranquil feeling.

Mr. Kitty looked across the shore. "Did we make it? Is this the gateway?"

"Yes!" answered Dair.

They travelled across the coast as Mr. Kitty recognized the hexagon columns pushing out of the earth. "What a natural wonder this is, so beautiful; how could nature form such a marvel as thousands of hexagonal columns towering out of the planet, creating a bridge out into the sea?"

"These columns connect worlds; they are in sync like wave peaks connecting and maintaining frequencies," said Dair.

The three settled into a corner to get out of the wind and off the water.

"May I ask how these rock formations happen? It is very unusual, indeed!" said Mr. Kitty.

"They are not as uncommon as you think. They have been formed over the years, bridging all three worlds. Lava pressure creates pillars as a result of powerful energy vibrating and pushing its way out. The columns are shaped as they are pushed up; portals to the underworld are scattered worldwide."

"Why would you need to separate the underworld from the other two worlds?" asked Mr. Kitty.

"One of the underworld spirits is causing chaos, and he has been confined to the underworld because of his destructive, power-seeking ways. This spirit must be contained to save both your world and ours," said Dair.

"Is the underworld connected to my world?" asked Mr. Kitty.

``Yes! And it is not impossible to find a passage," said Dair.

"As you have witnessed, we are also connected to your world, and Ireland's island reflection is very similar. We are connected through the energy of the light grid and the laws of electromagnetism. Your frequency is next to ours. This interconnected trilogy of universes reaches a climax here. We are the original two universes. The third universe was created to initiate a sense of time change in the three universes. We can observe change and energy transfer using existing science. Old sprites became hungry to control power and occupy space over time. This threatened the universe's stability as a few tyrants attempted to gain power and disrupt the ecosystem. Finn took control of the power-hungry Balor, trapping him in the now-known underworld. It has a few strong personalities," said Dair.

"So how does the stone come into play?" asked Mr. Kitty.

A low-toned, tired-sounding voice spoke: "It's the original spark where all life began when the beginning of time began," Finn said.

A giant of a man came out from the shadows behind a tower of stone columns.

"Now, what brings a woodland fairy, a cat, and my brother in arms...?" he said, smiling at Dair. "To my grave."

Chapter 4 Finn McCool

Tradition is a story told to celebrate a version of the truth,
clouded in mystery to balance the forces.
The matter of stone is heavier on the soul than the spirit.
Sharing in everyday experiences eases the weight of responsibility.
A tower with no ceiling
or a wall without boundaries
will entrap the soul from embracing its light.
The cage of the ego constrains impedance even more.
The struggle will lead to self-destruction.
The true nature is to be of limitless energy for enlightenment.
The spark resides in Mr. Kitty, allowing it to bond with the spirit
stone.
With grace and curiosity, he will find he already has what he is
looking for.

Finn lit a fire on the beach as the four chatted into the evening. It was a beautiful night as the sun set; Finn's fire had magical blue flames. He cooked some salmon and root veggies Mr. Kitty had never tried, but he choked them down to appease his host.

"That's a curious fire you built, Finn," said Mr. Kitty.

"It's a Druid fire. It holds an innocent and divine knowledge. I don't light the fire much anymore, as most nights are spent alone, protecting the Gateway. But it warms my heart to see it and have company. What brings you three this way? I don't think it was to come and eat salmon with me," said Finn.

"Dagda has approached us," said Dair.

"I felt his presence. What news does he bring?" asked Finn.

"He asked us to find you because you may be able to help us on a mission of critical importance," said Hazel.

"What journey has he sent you on this time, Dair?" asked Finn.

"Brace yourself, Finn; terrible news, as if you didn't have enough on your plate," said Dair.

"Don't hold back."

"The stone has been stolen," said Dair.

Even in the darkness of the evening, you could see Finn's face drop and almost turn pale.

"I have been distracted; there has been so much activity here with Balor. I feel his presence on the other side of this passageway; I have forgotten about protecting the person who protects the stone. This is my fault," said Finn.

"No, this is not your fault," said Dair.

"I let people down," said Finn.

"You haven't let people down. You have protected us for a long time. You can't do it alone," said Dair.

"What choice do I have? Our security depends on keeping the stone away from Balor. If Balor is contained, who would have been inclined to steal the stone, and what are they doing with it?" asked Finn.

"If you don't mind, who is Balor?" asked Mr. Kitty.

"He is an ancient sorcerer of the Fomorian race who roamed this land before the desire for power overcame him. He believed he should rule all three lands as new races emerged. He lost an eye due to his curiosity.

"He created potions for death with three friends, but some got in his eye, causing him to lose one of them and helping him discover dark powers within his grasp. His desire for power outgrew the rest, and paranoia overcame him.

"He killed his race, and the desire for more power grew. As he killed his race, he absorbed their energy, and they became part of Balor's energy. With each kill of his race, he grew more powerful. Once he killed his family, Balor was not who he once was. His whole race is in one conscious set of control of everything.

"He evolved into a Cyclops giant bigger than me. I was around when the Fomorians were still a peaceful race. He became too strong over time, and his focus shifted to the island's heart. I had to make moves and make the stone disappear, and had it protected until now," said Finn.

"Balor is evil. He lost all respect for life, even at the price of his own family," said Hazel.

"You mentioned you have Balor contained. Where is he now?" asked Mr. Kitty.

As he said this, they could hear a shallow sound, barely audible as the beach shook from the earthquake.

"He is trapped in the underworld, where the root passage that connects all three worlds is underneath our feet. I have helped put all these columns in place to block the pathway from the underworld to this world and the other world," said Finn.

"I fought him for sixty days until we could no longer resist. I saw a moment of weakness and managed to trap him since I could not kill him. He has regained strength, pushing the blocked pathway and making progress.

"He is moving toward the other world, your world, Kitty. I must destroy the bridge to block his progress further into your world. He is strong, and by killing all his kin, he has gained the power to turn his enemy to stone. Be mindful of his stare if you meet this unpleasant beast. Stay out of his eyesight. His senses have grown strong," Finn said.

"He has an eye in front of his head, and one inside that now glows so brightly from the trapped spirits of his people that it allows him to see three hundred and sixty degrees," said Dair.

"Just know, Kitty, even when you are behind him, be mindful that he may still have an eye for you," Finn exclaimed exhaustedly.

"In losing his eye, it seems as though his inner eye has developed a sense to be more in tune with his environment."

"More adept to view his enemies," Finn said, cutting Dair off.

"His vision may be strong, but his view has become foggy with greed and desire for power. If he gains access to the stone, with this powerful eye, he will be unstoppable; having unlimited power resources will take his destructive power to a new level, and life will never be the same... for all three worlds," Finn said.

"I have come to see adventure and new places, not to find out that a powerful, destructive Balor, the monster giant with an evil eye, is out to control and possibly destroy my world," said Mr. Kitty.

"Kitty, I'm sorry I bring fear to your heart. I had no intention of scaring you, but you asked, and I told you the truth. This is a burden I have been carrying for thousands of years," Finn said.

"The beast grows stronger, and now the stone is missing?" Finn felt frustrated.

"Dagda has entrusted the safety of the spirit stone to us, Finn...He believes you have information to share with us that will help us track the stone. Where was it last hidden, or whom have you confided in to protect the stone? They may have information to share," asked Dair.

"I have put all my trust in the one I believed was best for the job to remain hidden and to be held by someone who would not take advantage of its power. He kept the treasure for many eons, which may have been a considerable challenge. I am surprised he hasn't found me yet to tell me it was stolen. I hope he is okay," he said with sadness.

"Who is it?" Hazel asked.

"The one they call Runda!" said Finn.

"I heard of his legend, though I have never seen a Leprechaun. I was starting to believe they are not real; they are just fable stories passed down so long that they became folklore and mythology," said Hazel.

"He is very tricky; he moves here and there as quickly as a thought. One of his pleasures is taking in the beautiful sights of rainbows. He is old and wise, but simple pleasures can still attract his interest," said Finn.

"I can't tell you where he may be, or where the stone is. I'm sure he will be focused on finding me here. I will stay here to secure the Gateway. If he shows up here, I will send him in search of you," said Finn. "He will find you easier than you will find him."

"Could be anywhere, then," said Mr. Kitty. "At any time," said Dair.

"I know he has spent time in Cong or the area of the Ring of Kerry," said Finn.

"Cong!" Hazel continued, "That's my home."

"Yes. I knew you would be surprised by this," said Finn.

"How have I not known that a Leprechaun frequents the home of the woodland fairies?" said Hazel.

"He is very secretive, as you can imagine. He has the valuable treasure of all three worlds. His responsibility is great; he must remain hidden even to the point of turning to legend and folktales.

"Suppose you contact Athair, King of the Woodland Fairies. He is the oldest and wisest fairy in Ireland and may have a clue about finding the impossible. Hazel, please extend my respect to Athair. I have not seen him in a very long time and miss seeing my friend," said Finn.

"I will indeed, Finn. I know he has much appreciation for you as well. He has many stories to tell of the Great Finn McCool," replied Hazel.

"We have had many adventures together," said Finn.

"I was sure he was embellishing and telling fables, saying you two were on dangerous missions and escaped death on several occasions. He often tells the stories in which you have come to face Caoranach, the mother of all demons," said Hazel

"Oh, yes! The stories are inflated, I'm sure. Caoranach will surface again. She is malicious, feeding the fire, egging on Balor over the years, and using trickery to mislead those fighting to maintain stability in our system.

"We have had to come face-to-face a few times, and she has had a vengeance against me since I banished her to Loch Dearg.

"Athair and I combined music of the old way and put a spell on the lake to trap and limit her ability to roam the land, wreaking havoc. I haven't thought of her in a long time; she may be someone of interest who stole the spirit stone to get back at me. I have made an enemy in her, and she may want to sabotage me.

"Keep your eyes peeled on your travels, and watch your back. There is a lot to appreciate here in Ireland. It is a bridge to the different worlds, but times have changed. I maintained peace for a long time. I am tired, and my enemies may look to remove me from the peacekeeper position. Now, they are looking at controlling more than *Tir na nOg*; I am the Gatekeeper.

"If I were you, I would focus on the role my father has set for you. Rest well tonight and get an early start tomorrow, as time is threatened and critical, and we may run out of peaceful days. You should start heading south towards Cong and the Ring of Kerry, being mindful of Rainbows to find Runda," said Finn.

The four became quiet. Mr. Kitty had too many questions, but he thought it best to keep silent as he drifted into a disturbed sleep, concerned about the dangerous journey ahead.

Chapter 5 Kara DeFarraige

Hold onto calm bliss in the choppy water
Love and divine friendships will build from the honoured path
No moment is forsaken
With bravery, partnerships will develop.
A key to the known is respect to be shown.
Such a gift is a symbol of trust,
showing the innocence in devotion.
A simple beginning could grow into an impactful momentum
necessary for overcoming a challenge.
Grief may be present during a friendship,
But the support needed to endure is the present.
Land and sea are a bond required for each to survive.
Without working together, the fire will tear apart both,
and they will never be able to house the world for life.

Mr. Kitty woke early from a restless sleep. A great deal had happened over the past few days. He had been second-guessing his decision to get involved in a mission not only to save Ireland but to save three universes bound together in the science of nature—a peaceful balance that, if the connection was disturbed, could mean instant destruction and rebirth to all that lived in them.

Dagda confided in Mr. Kitty to join the mission with all the cosmos' wisdom. He saw something in Mr. Kitty that would benefit the mission and save life as they knew it. Fear and uncertainty have exhausted his brain, preventing him from getting any sleep.

Finn seemed to be sleeping quite well as he lay on the beach next to the smouldering ashes of last night's fire. Finn finally got a good night's rest and had some company to put his emotions at ease.

Mr. Kitty looked around for his friends Dair and Hazel. Though neither could be seen, he wondered if they had decided to travel without him because he might be a risk to the mission's security. Mr. Kitty only wanted what was best for life and maintained love as the dominant energy in his world.

Mr. Kitty left Finn to sleep undisturbed. He then went for a walk along the gateway columns, reflecting on the beauty that surrounded him.

Mr. Kitty trudged along the shore, exhausted and unsure of what he was in for. He had his head down as he walked along the beach, watching the waves crash into the rocks.

He missed his family, and while wondering where his friends were, he started to feel lonely and lost. Then, he heard a voice from behind a large rock in the water.

Mr. Kitty, usually very friendly, became more reserved and cautious as he looked around to see who was singing. The voice was almost angelic—a very soothing sound that comforted Kitty. Listening to this beautiful voice seemed to tickle his insides. He started to feel happy, like his family surrounded him.

We are an Island, a rock in a dream.
A power too significant for one spirit's hand
A line in the sand, no mermaid shall cross.
Save for true love's fate, to love and be loved.
All beings shall join each other at heart.
To do what we can through the darkness of night.
The morning shines bright; a shadow may fall.
We are all family, the heart of the land.
Our courage and our bliss shall guide the spirit home.
Do not give up face, should the gloom embrace.
Open up your flame; no sorrow will stand.
The Home of our Heart, Tir Na Nog

This sense of security overcame him. Listening to the voice was refreshing to his ears, and meeting the one who sang such beautiful melodies was like a hook luring him in.

He jumped up on the large rock on the shore from where he heard the music. He looked over to see a beautiful creature lying on the rock. But, to Mr. Kitty's surprise, the female did not have legs; she was more fish-like from the waist down.

He became very nervous because he was asked to be wary of strangers, not to mention that he had heard stories about merrows, painting them in an unpleasant light and trying to lure sailors into the sea. He was shifting his weight to his back legs to try to escape without being seen, but as he shifted his weight, some pebbles trickled down the side of the rock, grabbing the merrow's attention.

"Who's there?" the merrow asked.

Mr. Kitty did not move; he was just out of sight over the top of the rock.

"I know you are there; please don't be nervous."

Feeling uneasy, he stuck his head out over the top of the stone to look down on the marrow.

"I thought I saw a kitty," she said. "I have only seen a kitty a couple of times from a distance as they walk the shore for fish scraps. Please come closer."

"I dare not come closer. How do I know you won't lure me into the sea with your beautiful voice and trickery wordplay? I don't need to fall victim to your mischievous ways and attempts to eat me," Mr. Kitty said.

"Oh my," said the merrow, "very protective of yourself. It is good to be cautious about talking with strangers, but you have heard too many sailor stories about mermaids. I mean you no harm. My kind are gentlefolk. Those who speak ill of us are either jealous rumour-starters or have deserved the retaliation they receive from us.

"If attacked, we will turn the tables. We may be gentle, but if provoked, we are a solid force with which to be reckoned. We are far from luring drunken sailors; the last thing we want is filthy men," she said.

"Well, I must look out for myself to protect my well-being," said Mr. Kitty.

"You don't have to come any closer if you wish. I am excited to meet a kitty; few are on this plane. So when one walks along the beach, I must try to meet you.

I'm not sure what omen you bring. I have been sensing activity at the gateway, and now a kitty shows up. I am here at my father's request to monitor the gateway and report any strange or unusual activity. My name is Kara de Farraige, Princess of the mighty and benevolent Ri DeFarraige; his power is strong. Charity is great, loved by his merrow. We do as he pleases because he would give up himself for anyone," said Kara.

"My name is Kit Cat; my friends call me Kitty. I'm on vacation and have always wanted to visit this spot," said Mr. Kitty.

"My father recognizes that the gateway here is a threat to our well-being. Balor will destroy the land if he comes to the surface of the Ceo world. The sea, I'm sure, will follow; the land and sea need each other here. We surround you and protect the shoreline," Kara said.

"If we can be of any service to the Dia Maith Eagna, we give up ourselves for the greater good. My father and Dagda are great friends, but he worries about Finn protecting the Gateway. There is much respect for Finn amongst the Merrow.

"If the gateway were open, there would be no telling what horrible creatures would make their way here," Kara expressed.

"What do you know of creatures of the underworld?" Mr. Kitty asked.

"There are normal-tempered beings as well! Merrows travel between worlds freely and live in all three. But the underworld contains the worst possible monster, who killed all his people for power; there is no telling what he will do if he comes back here to face his oppressors. His vengeance may be great," said Kara.

"Why would he want to return here if he has his world?" asked Mr. Kitty.

"He is from this world. This world is the first universe frequency to exist; It holds the initial spark that carries all knowledge and the template of life. It is a source to channel energy," said Kara.

"What is the spark?" asked Mr. Kitty.

"I have never seen it; I heard it looks like the most precious stone, like its own tiny universe, clear as can be, perfect alignment in the palm of your hand. There has been a rumour going around the sea; the spirit stone is on the move, in the wrong hands," said Kara.

"How do you know it's on the move?" asked Mr.Kitty.

"There have been more storms lately. The last time the stone was threatened by Balor, the same mysterious increase of storms happened," said Kara. "My father is starting to worry about what is happening, as he believes the stone may be in the wrong hands."

"How does he know this?" asked Mr. Kitty.

"When the spirit stone is in the wrong hands, the surrounding environment is affected by the emotions of the one who possesses it, as energy is projected out," said Kara.

"My father feels the storms correlate with something happening with the stone."

"Do you know where the stone is?" asked Mr. Kitty.

"No...I don't have much to do with it. My father knows more but doesn't discuss it with me, and Eagna deals with this matter secretly," she said.

"I should inform Finn," Mr. Kitty thought out loud.

"You know Finn!"

"Yes. We just met, but Finn may be interested in the storms. Do you know where the last storm was?" Mr. Kitty asked.

"It isn't far from here. I could take you if you wish," said Kara.

"No, I have been travelling with two friends. I should try to connect with them. But if you could share where the storm was, I could pass the information along to find out," said Mr. Kitty

"It happened near Dunluce Castle; I'm here now. Why was there an unusual storm of the spirit stone near the gateway? The Merrow are worried."

"The spirit of the island connects us all. If abused, we will all surely be affected by the consequences of what energy takes possession of the stone; dark times will follow.

"Please, Kitty, talk with your travel mates. Mention my name so I can join your spirit circle to save Life. I will involve my father.

A merrow army will be a great ally in a time of need. We will all have to unite, because we are all affected," said Kara.

"How will I contact you? I'm sure you don't make yourself known to just anyone," Mr. Kitty said.

"Here, Kitty." She gave Mr. Kitty a necklace from around her neck. It was quite a beautiful stone of translucent opal. "Carry this with you. When you need help from me, this stone will draw my kindred to you. You can tell them I gave you this stone so you can contact me. Take it to the water and touch it, saying my name. I will feel the vibrations you are sending out for me. I will come if I can, or send someone I trust to make contact," Kara said.

"This is a very gracious gesture to give me your stone and volunteer your help during such peril," said Mr. Kitty.

"I may not know much of anything now, but if you are in Finn's company, you will need our help eventually. Finn will need as much help as possible. He has carried this burden alone for too long. We must all be responsible for the spirit of the Island," said Kara.

"Thank you, Kara. I will contact you. Peace be with you," said Kitty.

He turned and jumped off the rock, heading away from the shoreline to search for his travel companions. He returned to where he had left Finn, sleeping on the beach. Mr. Kitty saw him sitting on the edge of the cliff, overlooking the Gateway.

"Well, hello, Kitty. Where have you been off to? Have you seen Dair this morning?" asked Finn.

"I have met Kara DeFarraige, Princess of the Merrow; she has voiced her concerns on behalf of her father, Ri," said Mr. Kitty.

"What concerns do they share?" asked Finn.

"They believe a spirit of ill intention holds the stone. And I have not told her anything."

"What makes them believe this?"

"She said they have been recognizing a particular type of storm that Ri recognizes as the spirit of the Island—ill fortune sensed as the storm moved up the shoreline as far as Dunluce Castle," said Mr. Kitty.

"This is concerning, Kitty. Thank you for sharing this.

"I have to stay here to protect the gateway. You must find your company and make your way to Dunluce. I will send word to my father to let him know that storms have started. You excelled, although I don't know how you managed to capture Kara's interest. I'm glad you have contacted her," said Finn.

"She gave me a stone so we can contact her in the future," said Mr. Kitty.

"Perfect, Kitty, keep that stone safe, too. It is an exceptional stone that can protect and guide you in dark times," Finn said.

"Is Kara safe to talk to about what's happening?" asked Mr. Kitty.

"It's best not to yet; they are curious about something happening. They will be made aware of this in due time. For now, focus on moving forward. Continue being mindful of who you are talking to. However, Kara is indeed a friend and supporter of the cause. She is good to have contact with," said Finn.

Chapter 6 Dunluce Castle

Be mindful of the elements shown.
They will help gain knowledge from the known.
The language of the universe guides the path.
Science will not mistake a positive knowth.
The truth will echo at a frequency that respects its intent,
whether you are trying to hide the message or decipher the clues.
The effect will be consistent in its transcription.
Following the impressions in nature
will be openness to emotional instinct.
Past, present, and future echo love and pain,
Which need to find a balance for peace to remain.

Finn and Mr. Kitty sat on the shore, mystified by the news that storms worth investigating have blown toward Dunluce Castle.

"Well, no time for sitting around, Kitty," spoke Dair as he seemed to have come out of thin air with Hazel on his shoulder.

"Dair! Kitty has become aware that mysterious storms are off the coast at Dunluce, reported by Ri as spirit stone storms," said Finn.

"Where have you been?" asked Mr. Kitty. "I almost left without you."

"We were investigating as well, but it seems you have been doing a better job than us at finding a tip," said Dair.

"For a moment, I thought you had left me stranded here, not knowing how to pursue our mission," said Mr. Kitty.

"We will not leave you for long. Sorry, we didn't tell you we were leaving, but we assumed you were in good hands here with Finn."

"I am; I will get over my nervousness and feeling of being left behind," said Mr. Kitty.

"We should make our way to Dunluce, though," said Dair.

"I agree; if the spirit stone is near the castle, we should try to make our way there to get a quick jump on the thief," said Hazel.

"We should walk to the castle to keep our eyes open and see if we can see any suspicious activity along the way," said Dair.

"Finn, what's your plan?" Dair asked.

"I'm staying here to watch the gateway; if the thief tries to sneak in to contact Balor, I'll be waiting," Finn said.

"That's a good idea. What can I do for you? Do you need to contact your sister Brigid or your father?" asked Dair.

"No, they have already sent word that they will be here today to see me, and we will develop a plan. Once they have come to visit, I will send them to Dunluce to meet up with you. I won't be able to make it to the gathering tonight. Stick together and care for each other, for you are making a trail of hope. Thank you with all my heart for taking on this mission to save the spirit stone," said Finn.

"Take care, Finn; I'm sure we'll see you again soon," said Mr. Kitty.

"Be well, brother; you know how to contact me. If I can be of any assistance, call us," said Dair.

The three turned and started to walk toward Dunluce. "Be well, my friends," said Finn under his breath, not heard by his parting company.

"What a beautiful shoreline," said Mr. Kitty. "I love it here; Ireland is the most beautiful place on Earth."

"I agree," said Hazel. "I haven't been to many places outside of Ireland."

"Tell me more about *Tir na nOg?*" said Mr. Kitty.

"It's this place. It's the Ceo world to your world. All three worlds are connected, a balance like no other, a harmony that must not be meddled with," said Dair.

"I have always believed there is only my world. Why doesn't the other world know of your world, when you know our world?" asked Mr. Kitty.

"The spirit stone is a bit of a mystery even to me; it has ancient knowledge before *Tir na nOg* was even a place; the remanence of the great destructive force of the dark matter collapsing in on a universe in the past, crushing all remanence of the knowledge of a universe into a stone. When the stone shot out into the dark matter and ignited the beginning of a new universe, this universe, the spirit stone was a balance point for our world.

"*Tir na nOg* is the first timeline in the world; there was little change in the need for power. The stone was recognized by spirits even greater than Dagda as the means to create your world. This world existed long before your world, so we were aware of its creation. For a long time, the two universes had been in balance. There is little change. We live in peace. Time had little effect on the life that existed in both worlds.

"The luminous gods had an idea to create a third plane of existence with the stone's power. This third frequency of the universe established a solid foundation for the three of our worlds: first, *Tir na nOg*, second, your world, and third, the underworld. The stone had a profound effect on life, expanding the expansiveness of dark matter.

"Once the underworld was created, time began as you know it, steady and consistent change; *Tir na nOg* is the original plane of existence. However, since the creation of the other two worlds, constant change has begun, as time created a lifetime for spirits in your world and the underworld to evolve. We have developed a certain amount of experience with the transformation of energy forms. This has created the desire for power in a select few. If Balor gets the spirit stone, there is a potential to create or destroy universes," said Dair.

"Do you know who may have taken the stone?" Mr. Kitty questioned.

"No, we're not sure who would work with Balor; many creatures have evolved to desire more power. We are not sure why someone would take the stone for themself when Balor most certainly will be coming for it," said Dair.

They walked in melancholic silence along the cliff's edge. Mr. Kitty's sadness about what he had gotten into changed to excitement as they walked over a hill. The most spectacular sight came into view.

Dunluce Castle, perched high on a cliff above the rocky shoreline, was no ill sight to behold. Their pace picked up a bit as the excitement grew in Mr. Kitty's heart.

"I can't wait to see the inside of this castle. I have never seen anything like it," said Mr. Kitty.

"It is one of my favourite places to visit," said Dair. "I have been coming here for a very long time to meet Finn, Dagda, and Brigid. It is usually on a special occasion that I come here to celebrate or meet for personal business."

"Whenever Dagda comes to a gathering, you will be sure there will be food, drink, and music," said Hazel.

"That's for sure. Even in war, Dagda seems to have a way about him. When times are weary, he carries a bright-hearted, infectious mood, making you forget all the negatives in the world," said Dair.

"There doesn't seem to be much activity at the moment," said Mr. Kitty.

"I'm sure there is more activity on the inside," said Hazel.

Mr. Kitty and Dair walked along as Hazel sat on Dair's shoulder. The castle, sitting on the cliff, was so large that it looked more like a beautiful village hanging in the air at the edge of a vast ocean.

The court appeared to be untouched by the passage of time. It was beautifully well-maintained, with no cracks in the wall from what Mr. Kitty could see as they got closer.

Coming over the hill, Mr. Kitty noticed the beautiful gardens outside the castle. As they reached the entrance, the courtyards buzzed with activity.

The evening was setting in as the sun was soon hitting the horizon. The sky glowed as the reds and purples started to colour the heavens. There was no storm tonight, but a few cotton ball clouds, with a calm sea, blanketed in a mist also coloured by the setting sun.

Feeling weary and exhausted from a few days of travel, Mr. Kitty began to brighten up as they entered the castle yard, knowing their journey for the day was over.

"This place inspires me every time I see it," said Hazel.

"Warming the soul," said Dair.

"I have never seen anything like it," said Mr. Kitty. "This is the first castle I have seen, and I could not have had a better first castle experience."

"Hello, weary travellers," came a voice as they entered the main gate.

"Welcome to Dunluce Castle; I am Richard Og de Burg, Lord of this castle. Dair, so good to see you, my friend. It has been much too long."

"How are you, Richard?" asked Dair.

"I'm doing well. It's a beautiful evening to host such a gathering."

"Richard, I would like to introduce Hazel, daughter of Athair, King of the woodland fairies, and Mr.Kitty, wise traveller, pure of heart, from the other world," said Dair.

"Hazel, it's my pleasure to meet you; I have heard many great things about you. Your father has arrived; last I saw, he's in the great hall. A kitty from the other world. Most peculiar, and how did a kitty from a different world make his presence here?" asked Richard.

"I met Dair while travelling, and he graciously showed me the way," said Mr. Kitty.

"A talking kitty as well, my young sage. It is truly an honour to meet you. We have cats here in Dunluce, but none will converse," said Richard.

"Lovely to meet you, Richard! You have the most amazing home," said Mr. Kitty.

"Thanks, Mr. Kitty—make yourself at home; you are welcome anytime. I will have quarters made up for you tonight. But first, we will feast and meet with Ireland's finest company to behold. A few have already gathered, and a few yet to come; please make your way inside to fill your belly and rest your feet."

"Thanks, Richard; I sure could use a bite to eat," said Mr. Kitty as he turned to get inside.

"You will find plenty of food and drink in the main house," said Richard.

Dair and Hazel thanked Richard as they turned to follow Mr. Kitty through the gateway.

As they walked into the courtyard, quite a few people buzzed around. Mr. Kitty quickly felt out of place, and several people unintentionally kicked him to the side because no one looked down to see loved ones and friends.

As the dust cloud filled his eyes, he banged into the castle's wall. Unable to see, he opened his eyes and looked around, blurry-eyed, to see if he recognized anyone. He was sure he had seen Glic out of the corner of his eye, but when he reached the main house door to catch him and at least talk to a familiar face, Mr. Kitty had lost him.

Then he heard Dair call his name. As Mr. Kitty looked around the crowd, trying to find Dair, he saw them approaching.

"I would like to introduce you to a couple of friends who will be joining us this evening," said Dair.

Mr. Kitty looked up, the dust in his eyes, to see the true stature of a warrior with long, golden brown hair and solid muscle. He was not quite as tall as Finn and Dagda, although he was pretty close. He had a scruffy beard and several scars and tattoos. A dark cloak draped over his shoulders, pinned with a gold broach and firefly red stone.

If Mr. Kitty saw this man out of this controlled environment, he surely would stay out of sight, judging by the size and roughness of his character.

"Kitty, meet Lynx and Brigid, Dagda's daughter." Mr. Kitty looked over to see a beautiful, fair-skinned girl with red-blonde hair, wearing a lovely white crochet dress adorned with flowers. With flowers in her hair, she seemed to glow.

Mr. Kitty was sure it was the dust in his eyes, but as he looked up at her, the dust disappeared, and he felt warm inside.

They left him, and he felt nothing but love for her. If he had any worries, they would be gone.

"Pleasure to meet you, Kitty," she said.

Stumbling through his words, he said, "Purr..pleasure is mine, I'm sure."

"So this is the one whom Dagda has his confidence in?" Lynx spoke as he bent down to one knee to greet Mr. Kitty.

"I will do my best, Sir, to find the stone. I'm not sure I have much to offer, but I'm honoured to join your circle," Mr. Kitty said.

"I am at your service, young kitty! There is much mystery to what has happened, which will affect us all if it goes in the wrong direction; grace can work in many ways. I sense the light working," said Lynx.

"Thank you for your kind words, Lynx," said Mr. Kitty.

At that moment, Richard walked by. "Come, come, my friends; eat in here, fill your belly with lots of food and drink."

``You are a kind host," said Dair.

They all followed into the main house. Mr. Kitty was so impressed with the hall, which had one long table down the middle filled with food, a big fire burning in the massive fireplace at one end, and candles burning in the chandeliers.

"There you are, Kitty." Hazel approached.

"Kitty, this is my father, Athair. He is our Elder and wisest of the woodland fairies."

"Oldest maybe, but wisest, I'm sure, can be questioned," said Athair.

"Very honoured to meet Your Royal Highness," Mr. Kitty said, bowing.

"Please call me Athair. That is what most call me; I'm not much for formalities."

"Athair, it is; I hear you have met Runda?" asked Mr.Kitty.

"Ha Ha. Oh, yes, we are very old friends. However, I have not seen him in a very long time. We often meet up for an ale or two."

"How do you keep this secret even from your daughter?" said Mr. Kitty

"I will not live that one down. I kept this a secret for his protection," said Athair.

"You could have shared this one," Hazel said. "I have been a big girl for a long time," said Hazel.

"You are very special to me, but if I told you, and your brother's and sister's found out, it indeed would show my favouritism," said Athair.

"Come, Kitty, let's have a bite to eat. This food smells delicious," said Athair.

"I would love to join you. I have not eaten a solid meal since last evening with Finn," said Mr. Kitty.

Dagda walked into the hall, barely fitting through the door, while Brigid greeted him lovingly.

"Welcome, Dagda." Mr. Kitty heard a celestial voice float across the room. He saw a woman almost glowing white in a long white lace dress. Her long, flowing brownish-red hair was held back by flowers.

"I am Danu, for those who don't know me. Now that you have all arrived, I would like to thank our esteemed host, Aurther, for the delicious feast. All that is expected has arrived, save for two; he has been missing for some time. I have sent word throughout the land for the whereabouts of Runda, and Finn bears a heavy burden.

"Let us gather around the table as we feast and discuss this veiled spirit circle. A mission subsequently binds us. With our combined efforts, we shall prevail in finding the spirit stone and tracking the whereabouts of our mysterious confidant."

"Our secrecy, of course, is protected by Man Mac Lir," said Danu.

An elderly gentleman pulled back the hood on his cloak, seeming to come out of the air. He was an older man with a long white beard and pale, weathered skin. His cloak was a flowing blue, and Mr. Kitty was sure it was made of water.

A chorus of warm wishes from around the table and a big hug from Lynx seemed to brighten the sea god's face.

"Thank you all; seeing some old friends, family, and a kitty I have never seen before warms my soul," said Lir.

"This is Kitty, Lir," said Dair. "He is pure of heart, summoned from the other world by me. I sensed the stone calling, guiding Kitty to my roots. I escorted him to *Tig na nOg* and brought him to Dagna, who entrusted him to our circle."

"Well, my senses are not as sharp as before the age of time. A pleasure to meet you, Mr. Kitty," said Lir.

"Kitty is fine; the honour is mine," Mr. Kitty said, lowering his head.

"Oh, my! You are distinguished, Kitty. You are an excellent fit to sneak past many who will be watching for us. It's good to have you join us," said Lir.

Danu continued, "Welcome, spirit circle, our most gracious host Richard Og de Burg, Dagda, Brigid, Hazel and Athair of the woodland fairies, Man Mac Lir and son Lynx, of course, Dair, and Mr. Kitty. We send our thoughts to Runda, who protects the treasure, and Finn, who watches over the gateway.

"I want to bring to your attention that there have been mysterious storms in this location; it's too curious that they should have happened so close to the gateway where Finn is keeping Balor in the underworld," said Danu.

Just then, a ghost-looking woman glowed while walking through the castle wall, her hair moving as if floating in the water. She began to scream, an awful pitch sound that Mr. Kitty's ears couldn't handle. To hide from the noise, Mr. Kitty, terrified, ducked his head into his paws. Everyone else looking up took their hands off their ears as the banshee paused her screams to speak in a mysterious voice, heeding a warning to the room.

"Behold, the time thief looks to turn light to shadow.

"Death on the horizon for the treasure keeper."

"Kleena! Speak with us." Lir hailed, "What do you foresee?"

In hearing Lir, Kleena seemed to have changed from a distant, focused look to her face dropping in sympathy. She didn't know she was there and woke up in a room full of people.

By disrupting her focus, her energy dissolved before their circle's eyes.

Chapter 7 Spirit Circle

Doors are found in the fog,
and all possibilities are grasped like steps on a misty ladder.
Malleable with the light's construction to define the curious cat's
path.
The devotion of love for the journey
is more precious than the treasure.
The true gift of life is the love of the moment
and the hope of a brighter horizon.
To help those loved and cherished, the time shared.
The bonds strengthen as the circle is complete to create a stronger
net.
A life that is parted
is not lost but is now part of you, strengthening the connection.

Kleena, gentle as she is, brings a disturbing message to the spirit circle. Appearing out of nowhere before Mr. Kitty's and the spirit circle's eyes.

"Very afflicted, this message," said Danu.

"Lovely as Kleena is, I never look forward to her warning," said Lir.

"I agree; she didn't bring good news this time. Since we don't know where Runda is or who the time thief is, we should send a couple to Cork to see if we can find Kleena. She will be most willing to help us in our efforts to solve this mystery," Lynx said.

"I agree with Lynx; Kleena may not recall much of what she has said here or even know much depth to the warning she gives. But she is always willing to assist in our mission," said Dagda.

"I know Kleena well and am likely to find her," said Brigid.

"Finding Runda may be necessary at this time, for he is heading west, and we don't know if he will have essential clues. Saving his life will benefit all," said Danu.

"Runda is a good friend to me, better than any other, I'm sure," spoke Athair. "The eye does not readily catch him; now that he is vulnerable, I may assist in finding and showing him to another. He could be anywhere in Ireland. My gut tells me he may be close to his frequent stopping spot in Cong. If this warning is genuine, I am tempted to make my way tonight," said Athair.

"He has not crossed the vale yet," spoke Lir. "I may not be as sharp as I once was, but I don't foresee that he will go west for at least a few days. However, there is much uncertainty about whether anything can change after that. You do not need to hurry out tonight," said Lir.

"I believe that following the trail we have learned today is essential, but tracking the stone and trying to understand what Balor is up to should not be overlooked. *Tig na nOg* is speaking to us as well. Storms and aurora are clear signs of where the spirit stone is located. Tides can also be affected. An earthquake can be a distress sign, though Balor is also trying to return home, so there will be mixed signs there," Danu said.

"I will go to the underworld to see what Balor is up to and see if I can get any information from him. I know he will be suspicious of my visit, but it's long overdue for us to be face-to-face," said Dagda.

"You are not going alone," said Lynx. "I should also face Balor. He is my people. They were once a good race, misguided and blinded by power; Balor killed all of them, including my mother and siblings. It's my destiny to face him. He may have been my grandfather, but he no longer exists. His power, I fear, is too much for even him. He must be stopped, and I should be the one to kill him; I survived as a blessing of Lir. I should repay and save life from Balor's destructive way."

"You are brave, Lynx," said Danu.

"I believe it is an excellent plan to join Dagda in the underworld to confront Balor. This situation has become a greater concern to me than *Tir na nOg* has faced before; our entire existence is now threatened. The sound of a time thief turning light to shadow has me concerned. For the beloved Kleena to bring a warning of such seriousness is a possibility for the future. I will have to meet with the twelve luminous beings to discuss the significance of this circumstance. Dair, I would have you join me at the megalithic circle in *Tuatha De Danann* to summon them. We will need to gain their attention.

"It seems that our meeting has raised more questions. We are fortunate that, as anticipated, we have some leads to follow," Danu said.

"Brigid, you head to Cork or Glendora to speak with Kleena to see if she has any insight into the message she warns," Danu said.

"I will," answered Brigid.

"Dagda, you and Lynx are courageous, and we are very grateful that you will travel to the underworld to locate Balor and see what he's up to. Athair, your friend Runda also needs immediate attention, for he is in danger and may have some light to share. If you and Hazel return to your home in Cong, please attend to him.

"Kitty, I sense your fear and uncertainty about your place in all of this," said Danu.

"Yes. I feel I have little to offer," said Mr. Kitty.

"It is certainly not true for you to travel unnoticed here; you are difficult to sense due to your pure heart and coming from the other world. You have even more of a mask to Balor; you may be hidden. Therefore, you should join Hazel and Athair at their home to find Runda. For if they suspect eyes as you track Runda, you have a fair amount of stealth here, and it appears as though Hazel and Athair are just coming home," said Danu.

"I would be honoured to join Athair and Hazel to find Runda. It would be a dream come true for me to go on a rescue for a Leprechaun," said Mr. Kitty.

"This is a perilous time; be mindful and stay safe. We shall meet in Killarney a week from tonight, " said Danu.

"Please, Danu, I should tell you I have met a merrow, Kara De Farraige. She has mentioned that her father, Ri De Farraige, has been growing suspicious that the stone is in the wrong hands," said Mr. Kitty.

"Thank you, Kitty. How have you met a merrow?" asked Danu.

"I followed her beautiful singing on the shore last night. She is concerned for Finn," said Mr. Kitty.

"As are we all," spoke Brigid.

"She has said that the land and the sea coexist, and undoubtedly, if one is affected negatively, the other will surely suffer," said Mr. Kitty.

"Indeed, Kitty," Lir spoke.

"She has given me a stone to contact her if we need help from the merrow. She believes that a merrow army would be ready if we need assistance. The gateway goes into the sea. So, if it should be destroyed and opened, the merrow may be good allies to battle at the gateway to help Finn and the rest of *Tir na nOg*."

"Kitty is right, Danu," said Lir. "I will contact Ri and update him on what we know. The king of the merrow should be informed of what is happening. They also have a way throughout all three worlds and will be good to have in the spirit circle."

"Our mission is set; may peace follow us and bring us back together," Danu said as they talked into the night, planning for the uncertain future ahead.

Chapter 8 Brigid and Kleena

Islands of memories are washed out,
a torrent in a bubbling way.
Stone has stood the test of time
as if memories and emotional thoughts are stored in a rock.
What happened to subconsciousness
to create such a barrier to self,
how torn and sorrowful the experience had to be,
to overcome her fear and find peace from within.
The shadowy truth reflects inward antiquity
to create an outward experience.
With unsettled waves,
a vice attempts to define the edge of the mind's duality.
Self-discovery is a feeling and a response.

The spirit circle discussed strategies throughout the night. Kleena, Queen of the Banshee and Druidess of Love and Light, brought a dark warning that the timekeeper was looking to turn light to shadow, and Runda may die in the next few days.

This warning brought a sense of uneasiness to the spirit circle, and the news spread quickly throughout the castle and village, leaving them unaware of how the words seemed to have escaped the meeting so quickly.

The night became a social gathering, with the castle's people joining the feast. After the meeting came to a close. Dagda was undoubtedly one for social community, bringing everyone together and lightening the mood with good cheer.

Dagda eventually brought out the harp, which seemed to have removed all the fear and worry from Kitty and the room. After a few songs, musicians began to join Dagda, bringing in drums, whistles, and various string instruments.

Mr. Kitty thoroughly enjoyed his night. Becoming weary, he headed to rest his eyes, much earlier than the rest of the party. Meanwhile, the social gathering played music and conversed through the night until the early hours of the morning.

The sun was just about to peak over the horizon when Brigid stood on the cliff's edge, looking west out over the ocean as the waves crashed far below. A beam of gold light broke through the trees, cutting through the fog past her.

Brigid was a brilliant Druid, even before her time. She possessed skills beyond those of the average druid goddess. In a gentle yet profound way, her pure and potent light radiated from her more than from the average person. She was naturally born in the course of the wizard. Understanding the element was like a mastered instrument born of the fire of knowledge before taking form as Dagda's daughter.

Turning to face the beam of light, her robes caught by the breeze, she seemed to float into the wave of sunlight, drawing in the air for a moment as she glided along it, dissolving into the light and fog. The sun's golden rays turned into a mixture of gold, blue, green, and pink dust as the wind carried it away.

She formed in the middle of a Druid stone circle in the south of the island, west of Cork. Delighted to feel the warm sun greet her face, she closed her eyes to better sense her memories of being here. Dagda was always a kind and playful soul who loved to help Brigid realize her full potential. This was the first place she remembers translocating to.

"Is that you, Brigid?" came a voice behind her. Turing briskly to see Kleena.

"Welcome back to Dromberg; I haven't seen you in a long time," said Kleena, running over to hug her beloved friend.

Kleena is beautiful when not scaring beings with her dark predictions. She is dressed humbly in an earth-tone dress, slightly ragged, with dirt stains from working in the gardens. Her long, golden-brown, wavy hair hangs to her shoulders and is tied back in braids.

"Hi Kleena! It was much easier to find you than I thought," said Brigid, shocked at the coincidence of meeting Kleena.

"I came to the circle by chance. I have not been here for a few weeks, but I like to come up here to reflect. These stones help to give me insight when I have an unsettled feeling," said Kleena.

"What uneasy feeling are you having?" asked Brigid.

"I'm not sure, Brigid. I was at my place last evening. I just got home from a walk and lit the Druid fire in the backfield. I was feeling unsettled. I couldn't put my finger on it, as if there was a darkness within me, but not just me; I could feel the land calling out for help. So I lit the fire to ask the gods what I can do to help the land; when I am unsure what the problem is," said Kleena.

"Do you recall what they said to you?"

"No, but I had a vision," answered Kleena.

"What vision?" said Brigid, wanting to gain more insight into what Kleena had experienced the night she appeared before the spirit circle, to bring a warning from the known in her Banchee form.

"I could sense a shadow in the darkness; there was a pain that the shadow was feeling, an ache that could not be healed. A sense of remorse. I was curious and went into the darkness to search for the shadow.

There was a long tunnel with occasional untouchable windows. I felt pain when I tried to touch the windowsill. It may have been an apparition of a possible past or a possible future. But as I got further down the tunnel to find the pain of the land, I saw the light at the end of the tunnel. I didn't feel good about where I was heading; I paused to second-guess myself about going through the door with the light.

I asked the gods if they were still with me. I felt like I was going to die. There was a pain in my arm and my chest. I looked down and saw blood over my left forearm, and my chest felt heavy.

I remember saying I would die out loud, and there was laughter. *Yes, you are going to die.* A grey cloud overcame me. I don't know who the voice came from, and I never saw anyone; I just heard the voice.

When the grey cloud came, I asked about death and the shadow that haunts me, but at that moment, I recall seeing Man Mac Lir's face in the mist. He asked me to speak to him. I was disrupted from my dream, which was fine as it was becoming disturbing, and I woke up by the fire."

"What do you suppose it meant?" asked Brigid.

"I don't know. I haven't thought of Lir in a long time. Why he would pop up in my dream is beyond me. Maybe I should search for him, but I wouldn't know where to look if he requires assistance."

"Lir was with me last night," Brigid continued. "A group of us formed a spirit circle, and during our meeting, you appeared before us. Bringing chilling news with a dark omen." Brigid said, reaching out to touch Kleena's shoulder."What, really?" asked Kleena, shocked that she projected herself again to the astral realm.

"Yes. You brought a warning that the time thief looks to turn light to shadow, and death is on the horizon for the treasure keeper."

Kleena's face dropped, similar to the way it had sunk in last night's meeting, when Lir, as if, woke her from a dream.

"I don't recall appearing in front of the gathering or saying these words."

"We have some terrible news to share with you, " said Brigid as three white doves sang in a tree close by. Kleena looked over to listen to them as Brigid spoke: "The spirit stone has been stolen, and we fear the death you foresee is Runda's."

"Oh no! This terrible feeling is true, then; the land has been calling for help. What is the darkness that wants to turn the light to shadow?" asked Kleena.

"We also don't know what this shadow is because it is alluding to some of the most brilliant minds in *Tir Na nOg*. It must have a terrible influence over someone, and what is it doing with the stone?" asked Brigid.

"Could it be Balor? In the dream, I was going through a tunnel, and the light at the other end was unpleasant—possibly representing the underworld and Balor," said Kleena, having a vision of the light shining at her as she felt frozen.

"We have Balor in the back of our minds, but he is still in the underworld, and the stone is already missing. We are unsure who has the stone and who would work with Balor. His people are gone, save for Lynx, and he would never support Balor," said Brigid.

"What about the windows on the tunnel walls? Do you recall any visions of what was in those?" Brigid asked.

"I remember a small town. It changed to a stone house in the woods. This was when the pain in me happened. While another window was dark when I heard the voice say I was going to die, I remember the shadow. I don't recognize the voice, possibly slag, an extreme version of an elf. It was hard to tell, though, and the dream was somewhat fading; I was half-trying to forget, since it was disturbing."

"I'm sad that this is a suspicion; it was scary. I was hoping it was just a dream. Is there anything I can do to help?" asked Kleena.

"I don't know. We are still gathering information. We may need your assistance, since what happens will affect all worlds and must be dealt with here in *Tir Na nOg* before it becomes a problem for the other worlds," said Brigid.

"My three angels may share visions with me so that I can help those in need. If Runda truly is in trouble, maybe I was given a vision so that I may help him," said Kleena.

"The problem is that we don't know where he is," said Brigid.

"That can be a problem," said Kleena, not knowing what to say next.

"Athair, Woodland Fairy King, thinks that he will be near Cong," said Brigid.

"Well, let's make our way there," said Kleena, intrigued by a clue to what she was experiencing. She wanted to help Runda and discover more about herself.

"Are you sure you want to be involved?" Asked Brigid.

"I'm already involved; my three angels called me to be here," Said Kleena confidently, looking over to the trees where the doves spoke softly.

The three doves took flight and landed on the stones of the druid circle.

"They have spoken; we must find Runda and heal him with the love light," said Kleena.

"We will travel to Cong together, then. I will need time to prepare for my departure. The day is getting on, so we should make a fresh start at the crack of dawn to make the journey," said Kleena.

"Kleena, I can take you on the light so we can make the journey fast if we leave tonight," said Brigid.

"But I, too, have a secret to share. I think I saw Saoi. We can consult with the divine ox at dusk. He may be able to give perspective to what is happening or be able to find more insight into the darkness that eludes us."

"He is also the shadow, like a silent snake through the eclipse of light and darkness," replied Kleena

"What bad omen is on the horizon when Saoi makes an appearance?" asked Brigid.

"I am curious as well, I have spotted him off the shore cliffs; he's taking solitude in a cave," said Kleena.

"I have not met Saoi!" exclaimed Brigid. "What do you know of him?"

"He is a puzzle and mystery to me. His solitude has intrigued me, but I have never sought to find him; I have respected his desire for privacy. It is meant to be that we see him. Is it a coincidence that you arrived and I saw him off the coast? He does not just show up. We should seize the moment and take advantage of it to meet the shadow warrior of all battles that have been fought on the homeland," said Kleena.

"He has not been spoken about—nonetheless to be seen—in so long, he has become mythology. How did you recognize him?" asked Brigid.

"I'm not even sure it is him. I saw mist moving around the shore last evening, and I am sure I saw ox horns leading the way. His head and long body turn to mist for secret travel," said Kleena.

"His horns have obtained legendary status as a warrior. When the Irish were ambushed, Saoi would emerge from nowhere to fight and give the enemy his horns. If there is any threat to Ireland, Saoi will protect the island's security. He will likely know the spirit stone is missing and will track the movement." Brigid confirmed, thinking that if Saoi is present, the spirit circle can use all the help it can get.

"I think it is a good idea to find Saoi, he has a wealth of knowledge of dark energy and light strategies to overcome oppressors," said Brigid

"Come with me to Old Head. I was meditating there, and out of the corner of my eye, it was moving along the shoreline. My gut told me it was the divine Ox," said Kleena.

" Such a spirit will be a challenge to find, but with the two of us, we may have a better chance to meet him," said Brigid.

They headed off in a southwest direction; Kleena usually travelled in the company of three spirits: presence, health, and love. The three white doves took flight to follow them.

The three spirits have taken on other forms, such as appearing as butterflies, fireflies, or dragonflies. They are never from Kleena as she channels the spirits to help with health and well-being. The song of the three spirits can heal the ill.

Kleena feels she needs to go to Cong with Brigid to save Runda. Having the three spirits and seeing a vision of death. She took on the mission when she had insight into the well-being of another. A connection that draws her to explore whether her premonitions can be prevented.

"Kleena, do you ever remember the messages you bring to people?" Brigid asked.

"Not too often. The warning my subconscious shares is usually aware of someone going west, so it's frequently too late to save them. I believe I have warned Runda due to his contribution to the spirit stone.

I am a channel in most cases and try not to have any emotional connection. Most messages are a fleetin,g distorted memory of universal resin being lost in the cosmos. Forgotten dreams to protect myself," said Kleena

"Have you discussed in your meeting last night the consequences of the action of the stone getting in the wrong hands?" Kleena asked.

"Yes. There have been fearful things discussed, depending on who has the stone. The stone possesses seemingly infinite energy; all energy in the cosmos is said to align with the spirit stone. So this energy can be used to destroy or to flourish life.

The message you share of turning light to shadow makes us fear that it will be used to destroy the other world and the underworld, to bring back the original spiral of energy for a timeless *Tir na nOg*. But why someone would do this, we are unsure," said Brigid.

"If the stone is in the wrong hands, it could destroy the one seeking to abuse its energy and wipe out its existence," said Kleena.

"It is a widely organized energy holding its place in a perfect grid of all the universes. The power must be used with extreme caution and a profound understanding of the universe. Otherwise, it could work against you," said Brigid.

They made it to Kleena's home to gather a few supplies. A peaceful log home that blends in with its surroundings. Accented with wild flowers and moss growing on the outside. Large windows keep it naturally bright on the inside.

"We should not waste much time," Kleena said, walking out the door.

"Come over to me, Kleena. We can travel on light waves to reach our destination quicker," said Brigid, reaching over to Kleena.

Kleena reached over to touch Brigids' hand; as they made contact, they turned invisible to the eye, streamlining on light waves in the direction of Old Head.

It seemed like no time had passed, and Brigid guided them to the cliff's edge. "That is great!" exclaimed Kleena. "I should be practicing how to streamline. That is a great way to travel."

"It takes time to learn, and patience is key. It came easily as my birth suited me with the ability, but learning is also possible," said Brigid.

"Let's walk along the shore. I saw it just over there," said Kleena.

Chapter 9 Dagda and Lynx

Impel, using a circling approach
without using the eye,
spans dimensions in an orderly manner.
The vision shows a torrent of experiences to those on the island.
Shared empathy binds our force
to embrace common approaches and goals.
We are an island; No stone stands alone.
Peace to the souls who have struggled in pain.
The community's support can ease it.
We must strengthen bonds
to continue to celebrate our traditions.
Cultures coming together open the view to the truth;
One flowing spring travels in several directions.

Dagda and Lynx walked along the shore to the gateway. It was early morning. The air was still; blue skies and heavy waves crashed upon the beach. They approached the pillars and found Finn fast asleep, leaning against the hexagonal rock tower that rose out of the earth.

"Should we wake him?" Lynx asked. "I don't think it will take much to stir him; he will likely wake to any movement around the gateway."

Lynx and Dagda walked up the hexagon pillars, and Finn reacted to the movement by pulling a sword out and aiming it at Lynx's neck.

"I'm sorry, my friends."

"You must break, Finn. It will soon be time for a change. You can't live here without a good rest," Dagda said.

"I'm sure you are right. My senses are dull, and exhaustion clouds my brain."

"Have you sensed any movement from the gateway?" asked Lynx.

"I haven't felt much here. I know he is there, though, planning and waiting for me to be completely exhausted.

"I'm happy to see you both, but what brings you here?" said Finn.

"We are going to the underworld to face Balor. The council has agreed it is time to see his position and intentions. Is there anything you need, brother, before we leave?" asked Lynx.

"Nothing for me, just be safe; I know this will be difficult for you, Lynx, facing your family under difficult circumstances," said Finn.

"I fear facing them; it has been quite long since I have seen Balor. I don't think I see them as my family any longer. But mixed feelings of my parents have a spark of light in that evil eye."

"Open your heart. When you face him, your instincts and gut will tell you his intentions toward you. Be mindful; you are the last of the Fomorians. He will likely want to kill you to complete the full potential of his power. So my advice is not to let your guard down or your back to him," said Finn.

"You need to bring back the old man," Finn said light-heartedly as he looked over Dagda.

"Don't worry about me, Finn. I will be fine; I have the grace of the luminous ones on my side. They will have a guiding light for me even in the darkness," said Dagda.

"I wish I could join you, but I shouldn't leave this side of the gateway, knowing the stone is still in *Tir na nOg*. I won't give the thief a chance to escape to the underworld," said Finn.

"We will face Balor if you have faced him enough. We will track him and discover what he's up to," said Dagda.

"Peace and love, brothers," Finn said as Lynx and Dagda walked to the top of the pillars for the trip to the underworld. "We'll see you soon."

Standing on the highest point of the posts, a white light with a hint of pink and purples surrounded them as they descended into the stone like they were going down an elevator.

Their surroundings became foggy and dark, and they felt as though they were falling into a void, becoming weightless. The feeling changed to being rushed upward through the darkness, like buoys floating up in the ocean, becoming light around them. As their surroundings came into focus, they apparated out of the gateway to stand on what looked like the same spot in *Tir na nOg*.

"Now that we are here, Dagda, where should we go?"

"Balor is easy to sense for me with the guidance of the luminous ones. He is straight out in the Newgrange direction."

"Great; let's have a light stream to discover what this monster is up to."

"I can't advise that we ride light waves now. Balor is strong. He will recognize my presence if I make such waves, and yours, too. He is likely very attuned to your presence. He wants you to find him, but we should approach him slowly. I don't know his exact location. I just see the direction."

"Okay, what do you suggest?"

"Good, old-fashioned walk; I gather it's best not to make Balor know we are here."

"Walk it is, then, Dagda."

"Let's not delay; we have a long day ahead."

Dagda and Lynx scaled the cliff to begin their walk south. The underworld was very similar to Ireland, which they had come to know and love, and the difference was the frequency radiating from the stone.

The island appeared very similar, but the beings living at the three frequencies were different, and the laws varied according to which world one occupied.

Dagda and Lynx were built for endurance and battle; they were rough around the edges, but steady and sturdy on foot. They were heavy on their feet, and Balor could easily track them. If Balor had known they were in the underworld, he would have headed them off directly.

Lynx gazed out at the horizon to the south as they walked for hours, mostly in silence. They grew tired and weary, exhausted from thinking about what they could expect when encountering Balor.

Lynx's head was becoming foggy, and he needed water. As he walked on, he could hear the fierce and determined shrieks of conflict, almost like wild animals fighting over the reminiscence of a meaty kill.

"What do you suppose that is, Dagda?"

"Pooka!" Dagda said with confidence.

"What ill fortune do they bring or give warning?" Lynx picked up his pace as he climbed over the hill and down to the Bush River.

Although the land may have been the same, the people and beings were different, so the housing and population varied between the underworld, *Tir na nOg*, and the other world. The goblins' screams and eerie chatter became louder as Lynx descended the river.

Maybe half a mile from the river, the shrieks fell silent. Lynx paused steadily to track pack movement or other cries. Dagda stepped up beside the river when he turned to make eye contact with Lynx.

"Do you see anything?"Lynx knelt to gain a closer look at the tracking in the grass.

"The path leads down to the trees beside the river."

"I think we should find out what all the commotion is about," said Lynx.

"Not excited to track goblins, Lynx?" said Dagda.

"I want to see what is happening; we could help someone who has ill fortune."

Lynx stood without further discussion and followed the tracks.

Dagda, with a sigh, followed.

"Dead! They are frozen; stone dead!" saddened cries echoed as they made their way closer to the woods.

"Hobgoblin!" Lynx said under his breath, looking back at Dagda. He proceeded with a sense of caution, as Pooka had made a bad name for themselves, living as if to serve their needs in the moment.

Piercing howls crack the silence, as shrieks can be felt in the soul of the Pooka.

"Please show some respect for them; call them Pooka. They're not all mischievous." Dagda said as he leaned on a birch tree, feeling sad with personal respect for the devastating loss of the Pooka.

"They sound angry; proceed with caution, Lynx. They can be peaceful and good allies if you dare to approach the Pooka. It can be tough if they set their destructive ways on you, but it's better if they are on your side. We may not want to bring attention to ourselves by getting involved in something that may not concern us." Dagda said with calmness in his voice.

"Frozen! Dead!" They heard howling cries.

The battle had already happened; the Pooka had yet to fare well. Balor taxes through the countryside with no respect for those who get in his way. Leaving a path of destruction. As the Pooka are left to mourn the ones close to them.

"Shifty little buggers, the Pooka are unpredictable. Proceed with caution; we are unexpected and need not make any more enemies on this journey." Said Lynx as he pushed back the brush to make his way toward the village.

Lynx led the way into the woods, treading softly, followed closely by Dagda.

They heard the moans of sadness and the rustling of leaves as they moved through the woods.

"They'll pay for this! Whoever should stone us to death." Yelling one Pooka with a passion for justice, calling out for retribution.

Lynx could see dark-haired figures moving quickly from around what looked like a monument of stone creatures of various shapes and sizes. In proper form, there were horse-looking creatures, wolves, rabbits, dogs, cats, goats, and Pooka, short with horns, dark hair, and unpleasant to the eye.

The hiss of a polka close to Lynx felt like it was in his head.

"The damned are here! The guilty have returned to the site of their crimes, Sire.``

"No! We are not the ones who have committed any crimes," exclaimed Lynx.

"We bring no fear," said Dagda.

"Liars!"

A Dark-haired creature came out of the woods to face the two strangers. A large black stallion with long, curled horns, slicked-back, shining hair, and eyes with white light in the pupils, slowly stepped out of the bush to meet them.

"Why are you here at the perfect time to make you guilty of this crime?" Spoke a voice hiding in the shadow of the Dark Stallion.

"We are tracking someone who leaves death in its path," said Lynx.

"Your house has come to face the one we track. Can we see the crime you're referring to? A little black creature sitting on the back of the stallion with black hair, big ears, only about two feet tall, and a face closer to what a rabbit should look like, spoke.

"Dagda, of *Tir na nOg*, wisest of the mystics, is that you?"

"Sinsear, my friend? What ill fortune has been bestowed upon your family?"

"I fear it's Balor that has crossed paths," Dagda said calmly, confidently leaning in toward Sinsear, showing respect for the family.

They walked a little further into the woods to see a dozen Pooka frozen as stone, appearing to be fleeing from Balor.

"What evil has he noticed that he has to turn all these Pooka to stone?"

"It is beyond him at this point, I'm sure," spoke Lynx. "Fear of losing power has gripped his soul to destroy those he feels threatened by."

"This is our home. We were no threat; he walked in on us," Sinsear said.

"There is no excuse for this tragedy. Balor is evil and must be stopped," said Lynx.

"Please, Dagda. Do you have your harp close? Please heal them, make them whole again," asked Sinsear.

"I'm sorry, Sinsear, my harp has no light to undo what has been done here," said Dagda.

"Your daughter, she can bring them back to life!" said Sinsear.

"No, I'm afraid her power is limited to that of what Balor has evolved into."

Silence had overcome the cries. Some heads hung in sorrow, while others were raised to the sky. A lone voice spoke to the memory of the fallen Pooka:

"To the north wind that blows,
brings a torment of woes,
hide your eyes from the light,
at the mouth of the westward gate.
A rush of news that it is time to flee.
The light is a cold wind that only
stillness and timelessness understand.
May the love of the east
warm the souls of the frozen,
to enlighten their path and bring them to the elders.
The love of the past will gather in the night.
We are comforting the family after a sacrifice, making peace
tenfold.
Be at rest and never regret.
Peace be to our loved ones, " said Sinsear.

"Dagda, you must be our guide for what to do next. A power this strong must be defeated. I speak on behalf of Pooka to offer our time to rid the underworld of savages who look to destroy life in their path. My heart summons me at the time to do what is suitable for the underworld," said Sinsear.

"Thank you, my friend. I believe you are right. We all may need each other at this time," said Dagda.

"What can we do?" asked Sinsear.

"Balor is headed south toward Lough Neagh. It may be good to scout him. We will need a plan of attack, and when we locate him," said Lynx.

"A plan of attack?" said Sinsear.

"Yes," spoke Lynx.

"This is Lynx, grandson of Balor and only remaining Fomorian," said Dagda.

"Lugh! The one legend and mythology foretold in the death of Balor?" said Sinsear

"My name precedes me, I see?" Said lynx letting his cloak open just enough to see his chested armour and fiery red gem.

Sinsear's wonder shows on his face; he is mystified by such a sign, which must be from the gods.

"Yes, we don't pray much on average, but lately, we have asked the luminous ones to fulfill the prophecy. Balor has brought his destructive ways to a once-peaceful underworld and is now killing Pooka."

"Lugh and Dagda, we are honoured to have you on the Bush River. We will most certainly be your scouts." Sinsear said, bowing his head in honour of those who would avenge the suffering inflicted on the people.

"Please call me Lynx!"

"Truly sorry, Sir."

"That's okay; I don't want my name to get ahead of me. Balor can hear the wind speak." Lynx said as he looked up to face an eastern wind, as a murder of crows could be heard cawing in the distance.

"Stay with us tonight and get some rest. We will celebrate your company and our death; we can start early in the morning. You have had a long day, and it will soon be dusk."

"You are very gracious, Sinsear; how can we refuse your offer?" said Dagda.

Chapter 10 Mr. Kitty

Trust in oneself is necessary to reach one's full potential.
Excitement and distractions can cloud the mind.
But you do not have to remove the focus from who you are.
Nature is not forsaken;
It embraces the life force
and guides us unchangeably in its laws.
From the view of oneness,
nothingness evolves from one plus one equals one.
A Flood of love embraces the rainbow bridge
to share the spark necessary in dark times.
A life made brighter is affected by the connection of friendships.
The treasure is found in the presence of others,
a power obtainable from the subtle infinity.
Dark in its nature, so enlightened is the view

Mr. Kitty, eager to start his day, was at ease before sunrise; now, he could not settle his mind from the excitement of what his day might bring.

"A Leprechaun; I can't believe I may meet one today. Last week, my world was safe and regular. I was planning a routine vacation; today, my outlook on the world will never be the same," Mr. Kitty thought.

No one was awake as he strolled around the castle grounds, and there was no way he could go back to sleep. Walking to the cliff edge, he wanted to find a cozy spot to sit, looking out over the ocean, until he noticed life around the castle. Then he could meet with Hazel and Athair for breakfast before they made the long journey to Cong, the home of the woodland fairy and Runda's frequent stopping spot.

He was silent for quite a while, reflecting on everything that had happened over the last few days and taking in the beauty surrounding him. He could not help but think that someone was watching him. The party last night went late. Many people were around, so it would be unusual if someone else didn't take in the majestic coastline, since the sun was starting to crack in the east.

"I should head back to the main house to see if anyone is starting to gather," Mr. Kitty thought as he returned to the castle. There, standing not five feet from Mr. Kitty, was Glic.

"Hisss," Mr. Kitty let out with fright.

"Don't be afraid, Kitty. It's just me!" he said slowly, with a curl of his lip to show a half smile.

"Why are you creeping up on me?" Said Mr. Kitty, feeling nervous about being near this ill-defined elf. His stench sickens Mr. Kitty's stomach.

"I'm not. I just happened to stroll by the same time as you," said Glic as he sways and twitches a little as if it is out of his control.

"You could have said something," said Mr. Kitty.

"I didn't see you till you stood up," said Glic.

"I suppose. Has anyone started to gather in the Hall yet?" Mr. Kitty asked, hoping to diffuse the tension in the air.

"I haven't been inside the castle walls since the party started to taper off only a few hours ago," said Glic.

"Oh well, I should make my way," Mr. Kitty said, walking past Glic while ensuring he keeps his peripheral vision on him.

"What are you up to today?" said Glic.

Mr. Kitty felt unpleasant as a knot in his belly kindled a warning. He felt uncomfortable around Glic and worried he might be up to something.

"Not much," Mr. Kitty answered.

"Where are you going? Do you need some protection? *Tir Na nOg* is unlike the other world; you will need a guide," Glic said.

"I will be fine," Mr. Kitty answered, starting to feel annoyed by the questions.

"I know you will, but there are creatures out there that are not so pleasant to come face-to-face with," Glic said.

"That is for sure; I feel that right now," Mr. Kitty said.

"Hey, I'm just looking out for you, since you're new to the area," Glic said.

"I don't appreciate your probing questions; what are you up to?" asked Mr. Kitty.

"Just being friendly, my defensive little friend."

"Just being nosey where your nose doesn't belong," said Mr. Kitty. "Have you been in alliance with Balor?" Mr. Kitty said sarcastically, driving his claws in the dirt as he crouched down.

"Ahhh! That is a pretty loaded question you have there, you filthy feline; you better mind your tongue and not spread false rumours you know nothing about." Glic said, widening his stance, to balance himself offensively.

"A little hostility with that question makes me wonder."

"I'm adverse to you asking such criticizing questions."

"A simple 'no' would have been a good answer to a direct question," said Mr Kitty.

"Well, I don't appreciate your question," Glic said as he moved closer to Mr. Kitty, reaching back to place his dirty hands on a blade he kept attached to his belt.

Feeling threatened, Mr. Kitty backed up a bit to open space between them. He backed up to the edge of the cliff as rocks tumbled down to the rocky shore far below.

Mr. Kitty let out a low growl to warn Glic to back away as he prepared to fight for his life.

"Are you going to kill me? Is that your plan?" asked Mr. Kitty.

"It wasn't at first, but I don't appreciate your insinuations and the risk of spreading false information about me. No kitty from the other world is going to spoil my name."

"I don't have to say a thing. It seems you spoil your name," said Mr. Kitty.

"Your grimy, arrogant cat, I will have you pay for flapping your tongue."

Glic advanced on Mr. Kitty, pulling his knife as Mr. Kitty stepped aside.

"Hey, what's going on over here?" Glic was startled by the voice; at the same time, he tried to attack Mr. Kitty. Glic turned and stumbled over the side of the cliff.

"Oh!" Mr. Kitty sighed as he looked over the side to see if he could see Glic on the rocks, but he couldn't see anything.

Atheir and Hazel came to Mr. Kitty's side to comfort him. At the same time, Mr. Kitty peeked over the edge of the cliff. "I don't see him down there. Perhaps he fell into the water."

"Good riddance, I say," spoke Hazel.

"Hazel, mind your manners, we should still have respect for life," Athair said

"He tried to kill me. I don't know what his problem with me is. He snuck up on me and started asking questions, but I wouldn't answer. I asked him about Balor, and he tried to kill me," said Mr. Kitty, backing up for Hazel.

"My sense tells me to be wary of that sticky, foul creature," said Hazel.

"A great truth will flourish from a tiny acorn," Athair said, knowing that Glic knows where the stone is.

"We should set forth toward our destination. Only now, I fear that suspicious eyes and ears are listening. We will need a way to make it to our destination in secret. I know the place to make it happen," said Athair.

"Let's go back into the castle to discuss our plan, since there may be curious ears listening," Athair said, leading the way up through the thick grass, toward the massive stone castle. A small arch door at the castle's base opened to a staircase leading up to the main level.

Mr. Kitty, Hazel, and Athair returned to the main room, where they had met the previous evening. Stillness accented the room, as tall, thin windows let in a warm, sharp glow that edged the dust in the air.

Richard, an early riser, is in the room when they arrive. Vibrant as ever, always seeming to have a cheer about him.

"Good morning, my friends." He said, smiling.

"Good morning, Richard, how are you feeling this morning?" Asked Mr. Kitty.

"Very well, thank you for asking. I have prepared breakfast. Please make yourselves at home; it's been a long night with an early morning, and I must rest this weary mind." Said Richard, touching his heart and lowering his eyes to his company.

"Thank you, Richard, for being such a gracious host. You have been the most accommodating. Rest be with you; we will leave shortly after breakfast," said Athair, nodding in appreciation.

"May the spirit shield you through every step you take," said Richard as he bowed again and left the room, leaving the three alone at the end of the long table. They picked at various loaves of bread, fruit, and cheeses that Richard had spread out for early risers.

"Kitty, how are you?" asked Hazel, seeing him quiet and staring into space.

"I'm okay, Hazel. I'm just a little shaken by what just happened with Glic. I feel as though he is involved with whatever happened with the stone."

"I agree," said Athair. "We must inform Dagda and Danu of his curious behaviour, which seems odd even for Glic. I believe our confrontation with him is not over yet, and that is why we need to speak in private and require a portal to travel that will secure our privacy."

"Where will we go?" Hazel asked as she shoved another strawberry in her mouth.

"It's a long road to travel in the wrong direction, but I believe it's best to make this diversion to save Runda. Hopefully, we will find help along the way for speedy travel to Ballynoe Stone Circle," said Athair.

Mr. Kitty, Hazel, and Athair ate a full breakfast to prepare for the long day of travel. No one else showed up during their time at breakfast, so they cleaned up behind themselves and left Dunluce Castle.

"It is nice that the day is cool; the heat would make the journey much more challenging," Mr. Kitty awkwardly said, trying to talk about anything other than the dangerous journey ahead.

"It's time we hit the trail," said Athair.

"I agree," said Mr. Kitty.

"Let's get started?" asked Hazel.

"Since it is a long road, it is likely a two-day trek across the Island. We should plan to make it at least halfway," said Athair.

"We have kin near Randalstown on Lake Neagh," said Hazel.

"I believe it will be best to head south and travel along the River Bann for water when we need it," said Athair.

"That's a great idea," said Hazel, excited to see her family and friends.

"A two-day hike! I am okay with this plan, as long as you believe it's best for Runda," said Mr. Kitty.

"I do, even if we travel south to Cong. It will not secure our secret travel, and we may have to travel an extra day on foot. If we don't find help to travel to Ballynoe Stone Circle, at least I know we have kin at the halfway point," said Athair.

"I like this plan. I am excited to see the countryside and visit another mystic stone circle," Mr. Kitty said, stepping lightly, with a couple of pounces, before realizing he was doing it, so he regained his composure and walked more proudly toward their destination.

The three walked for hours, and Mr. Kitty had more stamina and was quicker on his feet, since the woodland fairies were not very big. They tired faster and needed a break from flying or walking. Kitty offered to carry them on his back as they headed south.

The sun was at noon, and poor Mr. Kitty was getting tired. The long journey felt daunting, dry, and tiring. His paw tracks were becoming more staggered as they walked over a hill to see a river.

"We should stop for a rest," said Mr. Kitty, licking his lips at the sight of water.

"Yeah, I'm parched," said Hazel.

Hazel and Mr. Kitty headed straight for the river and flopped right in it.

"Oh, you gotta try this," Mr. Kitty said with excitement. "So refreshing."

Hazel joined Mr. Kitty at the water's edge, sitting on a rock with her feet in the water, while Athair was not quite ready to relax.

Fearing Glic was on their trail, Athair left them for a break and went out alone to survey the area for any questionable activity.

"Hazel, may I ask you a few questions?" Mr. Kitty climbed out of the river to sit in the shade and lick his paws.

"Yes, of course," said Hazel.

"Have you ever met Balor?"

"No; there is always a warning of Balor in the area, and we do our best to stay clear of him. The trees whisper, and being of the woodland fairy, we sense the trees' warnings."

"What does he plan to do if he gets the spirit stone?" asked Mr. Kitty.

"I don't know his purpose; I believe the spirit will not let anything play out that it didn't plan on happening," said Hazel.

"What do you know of the energy that has power over this stone?" Mr. Kitty asked out of curiosity to know more about the stone and how it brought them to this point.

"The luminous ones know what happened before *Tir na nOg,* and experienced the elements before space existed. The stone was formed according to the laws of nature. The stone is the reason for our existence, as it is an ingredient of the space-time grid, opposing space and timelessness. It was forged from the destruction of a universe collapse in the distant past; it is timeless, so *Tir na nOg* was timeless when there was only one universe anchored here," said Hazel.

"Do the luminous ones show themselves here?" asked Mr. Kitty.

"They are timeless so that they can enter our universe. I have seen it. Their frequencies allow the universe to exist, and their light, love, and knowledge survive here. You need to open your mind's eye to notice the peaks and valleys coming together.

"Spirits like Dagda and Danu have just enough frequency to have all the knowledge that exists here and can slip through the edge of the universe, similar to if you dipped your finger in soap and then touched the bubble. Your finger will be allowed to enter the drop, and the bubble won't burst," said Hazel.

"That is wild!" Mr. Kitty expressed.

"I know you are of the woodland fairies, but how many other types of fairies are there?" Mr. Kitty asked.

"That is a complicated question to answer, Kitty, as, like any species, we evolved with variations of each. Depending on conditions, we generally define ourselves as spiritual versus the elements. We are divided into seven categories: Earth, Air, Fire, Water, Weather, Light, and Individual. We each hold our special talents or skills," said Hazel.

"How old are you?" asked Mr. Kitty.

"I can't say in years because I don't know. We can live a long life, but we are not immortal," Hazel said.

"Do fairies live in my world, too?" asked Mr. Kitty.

"Yes, of course, fairies live in all worlds, in all environments, though they are very private because they have been used under the control of oppressors in the past to force us to use our skills for an ill fortune. So we have lived secret lives and stay hidden from the eye, even in *Tir Na nOg.*"

"Then why have you introduced yourself to me?" asked Mr. Kitty.

"I just happened to be at the right oak where you and Dair came together. I have been visiting Dair for a very long time; if he was escorting a kitty here, then you must have a heart with no intention of harm or ill fortune to me. One of my skills is to sense danger, and a loving innocence surrounds you," said Hazel.

"Thanks, Hazel; I am so happy you trusted me and made me a friend. Are all fairies as nice as you and Athair?" asked Mr. Kitty.

"Unfortunately, not. There are many personalities in fairy nature, ranging from the extremes of both positive and negative to being mischievous, causing unjust harm to others to elicit a reaction. Our stealthiness makes us think we are invisible, which most are not; we are just good with illusion and camouflage," answered Hazel.

Athair returned after a short while with a mixed bag of fruit he had gathered from around the area.

We must eat and get back on the road; it will be good to use daylight to avoid travel during the night," said Athair.

After a quick lunch, the three returned to the road. As they travelled, less talk ensued, and hours became long.

They were still a couple of hours away from their destination, and the three were becoming drained by their journey when they heard a loud screech from a bird hidden in a spruce tree.

Mr. Kitty, tired, looked up with a jump in his heart, scared by the sound of a predator, as he saw a large owl spread its wings and drop down in their direction.

"Hide!" Mr. Kitty cried as the other two looked up to see the owl coming down with another call, this time softer. He jumped into a patch of gorse, a thorny bush. He was hoping to escape the unsettling clutches of the owl.

"Ahh! Ouch!" Mr. Kitty yelled, terrified of the owl, while getting poked with thorns.

"Kitty, it's okay, come out!" Hazel said, helping Mr. Kitty untangle the mess he had gotten into. Pulling thorns out of his back as he climbs out of the bush.

"He is a friend, distinguished General Alta," spoke Athair.

Slightly embarrassed that he had jumped into the brush, he tried to exit gracefully so as not to show his frustration to their guest.

Alta's broad wingspan slowed him down as he lightly touched down to greet Athair. Gently accented with armour, a silver and gold breast plate embroidered with a crest of an owl sitting on a key with a four-leaf clover on the end of the skeleton key.

"Hello, old friend; how wonderful to see you back in your old stomping ground," Alta said, dignifiedly.

Mr. Kitty's eyes widened in amazement as he wondered about this great owl.

"It does feel good to be home, but I fear I am not home for long," said Athair.

"To what pleasure do the woodland fairy and owl parliament have to bring you here?" asked Alta.

"We are travelling to Ballynoe at the call of Dagda," said Athair.

"Why are you going to Ballynoe?" Alta said.

"I dare not speak of it here; we believe we are being pursued currently and must travel unseen. So Ballynoe will secure our trail to our destination," said Athair.

"I see," said Alta.

"We, too, are at your word, Athair. I speak on behalf of the parliament to offer our services to Dagda's command and the mission at hand. I will take you the rest of the way, stopping to visit family and discussing how we can help in private. I will help you lose the eyes that are watching."

"It would be extremely helpful, for our mission is time-sensitive, and it would save a day and a half," said Athair.

"It is a pleasure to see you, my lovely Hazel," said Alta.

"Honoured as always, General?" said Hazel.

"Please, call me Alta. This may be a formal mission, but we are always on friendly terms. And who's this, blessed to travel with the king and princess of the woodland?" Alta asked, looking at

Mr. Kitty, who gazed at Alta wide-eyed at seeing the crest on his breast plate.

"Alta, this is Kitty," said Hazel. "He is a travel companion of Dair and the spirit circle."

"How do you do, General?" Mr. Kitty asked as he bowed.

"My mist, a talking Kitty! I do so to ensure peace and well-being for those who deserve it. A pleasure to meet you; you travel in good company," said Alta.

"I am lucky indeed to have met such fine folks," said Mr. Kitty.

"I look forward to spending the evening with you, but for now, let's get you home," Alta said.

Alta looked up, and two more owls floated down to join the company.

"I will carry Kitty the rest of the way; my two companions can take you two," Alta said, looking at Hazel and Athair.

"You are heaven-sent, Alta," said Hazel.

"It has been a long day; I look forward to seeing family and clearing my thoughts about all the information we have received over the last few days," said Athair.

"Let's take flight, then," said Alta.

All three climbed on the backs of the owls, and with a leap and a few flaps of the wings, they were off. Any eyes that may have been watching were lost.

Mr. Kitty felt at ease and amazed at the fortune bestowed upon him as he took in the beauty of gliding over the countryside. He knew he would be met by good company and the security of a good night's sleep at the other end of this exciting flight with the owls.

Chapter 11 Saoi

Light boats in unison shall pivot any obstacle.
Not knowing the future will obscure any view of the outcome,
but light shall shine from the potential to illuminate the path.
Strong will is a movement through the cosmos
In search of the key that opens a broader view.
The connection to see the dragon inside
is not just a grasp of the unexplainable reality,
but being part of something more significant than self.
The power to overcome the illusion of disconnect
is the subduing to the realization
that the warrior is fighting to find you all along.
The answer sought is the response looking to be found.
The pursuit of one is not without the other.

Brigid and Kleena met at the Drombeg stone circle when Brigid travelled south to find Kleena and investigate the message she had brought to the spirit circle further.

They came to light, appearing on the cliffs of Old Head.

"Wow! That is spectacular," said Brigid.

"You have quite the talent; I would love to learn how to do that," Kleena said

"I know you have it in you to achieve the same level of awareness in travel. Three essential skills for such a trip are self-awareness, including understanding of your surroundings, controlled breathing, and confidence in your actions. I can guide you in meditation once we have time to relax. But now it's time to focus on tracking the mysterious Devine Ox Saoi; I know he will have some knowledge to share about the current predicament," Brigid said.

"I have never searched for Saoi before," said Kleena. "I'm unsure where to begin; I just saw him by chance."

"I have been in his presence a few times when Ireland has been attacked. He moves like the mist in the wind, primarily unnoticed and by his plan. However, it seems he appears when the island and its people are in dire straits. I suspect that is why he has appeared now," said Brigid.

"I believe he is feeling the threat of bad things to come. I'm unsure if he will return to where I have seen him. But he was here between Old Head with movement west toward Seven Heads," said Kleena.

"Let's walk along the shore to see if we can see any signs of his presence," said Brigid.

"How do you get the mist's attention?" asked Kleena.

"I am not sure how to have him talk with us. If we don't see him by dark, we should not waste precious time tracking him and instead travel to Cong to find Runda," said Brigid.

"That's a good idea, since I'm not even sure if I did see what I saw. The memory is fading fast; it was only a vague glimpse of something, and my thoughts instantly took me to Saoi," said Kleena.

"It will be worth the delay if we make contact; otherwise, a few hours' delay will not matter much."

The two walked along the shore, mostly in silence, as they kept their eyes focused out to sea, scanning the horizon for fog or any disturbances off the coast and along the horizon.

"You said you have been in the presence of the divine before?" asked Kleena.

"Yes! A very long time ago," said Brigid.

"How did you come to be in the presence?" asked Kleena.

"Most Fomorians were peaceful people in the early days; a few ruined their name. Suppose we could change the fact that Balor was influenced by power. I believe they would have been an excellent resource for good. Balor murdered all of the Fomorians with ill intent. When Balor was in his early stage of gaining power, he had a few followers trying to gain control over our land.

They were moving from village to village, pushing their power and ignorance. They were a seafaring race that landed in a northern town and began killing the villagers. I had sensed the disruption in our ecosystem and arrived at the bloody scene as Balor and a few others were wreaking havoc for no apparent reason.

I came to their aid. At the same time, Saoi arrived and killed the Fomorians with his horns. He moved around the village like mist and would head on to the Fomorians, who would drop dead with holes in their body.

Saoi would appear to go right through his victims, like a ghost. Then, he wrapped around to kill his next victim. Once he saved the village, he did not chat with the locals or me. He was gone as quickly as he came," said Brigid.

"Where does he come from?" asked Kleena.

"Saoi is one of a kind, well known even to the luminous beings as a mist. He has contacted them to be an ally in the fight for what is right. He has been around as long as the luminous ones, though he came to consciousness separately and can travel freely to all three lands of this universe and other universes," said Brigid.

Kleena sat on a stone overlooking the shoreline. Keeping her eyes focused as her mind wandered. She drifted into the beautiful colours of the sky as twilight seemed to linger in a timeless moment.

Brigid sat next to her and looked out at the rocky shore and crashing waves, feeling the uncertainty of the road ahead and wondering why anyone would want to create chaos when peace was so easy.

"You mentioned the Fomorians were good. How did it come to this with Balor?" Kleena asked, trying to keep the conversation going, as she felt she may have sidetracked Brigid from her path, to chase the mist in the wind.

"They were early seafaring settlers, looking for peace as well, needing food and resources, as their island settlement was quickly becoming at a loss to keep up with the demands of its people.

However, the people of Ireland felt threatened by the new settlers, who gave them a hard time and even tried to chase them off the land; nonetheless, the Fomorians settled.

"Four of them, including Balor, were unhappy with the pushback. They started to brew poison to kill those disrespecting their people.

Balor was a victim of his circumstances. Splashback from his evil brew caught his eye. Instead of killing him, he grew paranoid of his friends, and fear overcame him as he became increasingly suspicious that they would overthrow him.

Balor killed his three partners. He must have discovered a new power when he killed his own. So he continued killing the rest of his people out of pure paranoid suspicion, fear, and likely greed for power," said Brigid.

"Is there a way to kill Balor?" asked Kleena.

"It is foreseen that he will go down, but the future is becoming foggier and less predictable. The problem is that most beings turn to stone in his presence. So hide if you should ever meet him," answered Brigid.

"There!" said Kleena. "Did you see something?"

"No. What did you see?" Brigid stood up to get a better look around.

"A distortion of the waves, just off the shore," said Kleena.

Both paused momentarily to scan the sea, with no success in seeing anything.

"I'm sure I saw something," Kleena said as she moved closer to the cliff's edge to have a better view of the shore, squinting as she looked out at sea. Unable to see anything suspicious, she turned to Brigid to move back away from the cliff, but the edge broke away, twisting her ankle and causing her to lose her balance; she fell to her belly as she slipped down, and the land continued to slide away.

It happened so quickly that even Brigid did not react soon enough to grab hold of Kleena. She slipped off the edge, screaming in fear of the long drop to the rocky shoreline. She managed to grab hold of a weak root sticking out of the side of the cliff, letting go even further to drop her another five feet.

With her grip becoming more vulnerable, she called out, "Help!"

"Hold on! I need to grab something to reach down. I can't float down and lift you; I will not be strong enough. The sunlight is fading quickly," Brigid said.

"I don't have time. I am losing my grip, and this root will not hold," Kleena said as she slid another foot, losing her grip and footing as rocks and dirt fell to the rocky shore.

"I will be right back," Brigid yelled as she went to grab something to throw to the side to pull Kleena up.

"No, wait," she cried. "I'm slipping." The root pulled out at that moment, and she swung down, holding onto it. She managed to get down to a level where there seemed to be a cave on the side of the cliff.

"Kleena, where are you?" Brigid called.

"I landed in a cave; I'm safe for now," Kleena answered.

Brigid walked to the edge of the cliff. Since the sun was setting, she needed to be more stable when climbing down the side of the cliff.

"I'm going to find a rope to pull you up," said Brigid.

"I'm okay; I'm not going anywhere," said Kleena.

She surveyed the cave in which she had landed. "Let's see if we can scale the side of the cliff back up to stable ground."

"I'm not sure I am going to attempt the climb out of here; oh, what mess have I gotten myself into?" said Kleena.

"You could also ask what mess has found you?" a voice spoke.

"Who's there? I have friends coming for me."

"I'm of no harm; I was just inferring that the situation sometimes finds us rather than us finding it."

"That does not help my situation," said Kleena.

"No, it does not; you have come to my space. I should be asking who you are?"

"I am Kleena; please show yourself."

"Mmm, Kleena, the druid banshee who foretells possible futures."

"How do you know me?" Kleena said suspiciously.

"I know you! Spirit of the known."

"My friends should be here soon. Keep your distance, or you shall meet a most unwelcome ending."

A low laugh echoed through the cave. "I am of no harm. I am here to protect you. Remember, the situation has found you."

"How did you know, then, that I would be here?"

"I am all possible futures; the last week has become less predictable, and fewer possibilities are proceeding as time is closing in, the apex of certainty versus uncertainty, and you are here regardless of what is happening. Why do you seek the Divine Ox?"

"How do you know that?"

"I am the one you seek, the shadow of the shadow. I, too, am from the known. But I have not forgotten who I am, as you do. I have always been and will always be. Time has hidden me, but my awareness remains perpetual, undisturbed by the laws that affect others," said Saoi.

"What do you mean, I'm from the known?" asked Kleena

"You stem from the root of roots. For many years, you survived unfazed, knowledgeable of all the secrets of the spirit, seeing and warning people of their possible demise.

"For this, you have become attached to the living and descended to live as they live, being reborn. Your gift has attached to you, and you continue warning of death on the horizon, less controlled and much forgotten, but you remain connected to the known."

"I am the known?" said Kleena.

"Yes," he said as the shadows started to pull away from her surroundings, turning from darkness to a pale blue, purple, pink, or whitish hue, and consolidating at the back of the cave, where a massive ox was visible, four times the length of a typical bull. As the head and body took shape, he continued to show an aura of the same colour with white fur.

"My heaven, you are Saoi; am I hallucinating or dreaming?"

"Yes, and yes."

"So this isn't real?"

"It is genuine, as you are real and your dreams and consciousness are real, being connected to the known. We are the same; there is no dissociation between us. So, why have you reached this point? To seek guidance from me?" Saoi asked.

"As you are likely aware, there are dark times ahead; I seek you to help interpret what is happening and how we must overcome destructive forces that have taken possession of the spirit stone," said Kleena.

"I know the spirit stone, and the hands that have taken it, and for what purpose," said Saoi.

"This is good news," said Kleena.

"It is news to you; it is neither good nor bad that the knowledge exists to you. Uncertainty and time will decide the outcome," said Saoi.

"Well, someone has stolen the stone; this is bad news. Who has taken it?" said Kleena.

"The stone is in sticky hands; they have no intent to do anything with it, but will attempt to deliver it. This is why it has not succumbed to the universe's balance, a misguided dark elf who goes by the name Glic," said Saoi.

"Glic? Well, I don't know him. Who is he delivering it to?" asked Kleena.

"Balor, as I'm sure you're aware."

"What will he do with it?"

"It is difficult to tell; this is close to a meridian, and change is happening. He may have false beliefs in what the spirit stone is capable of, or he does know and is willing to see what happens," said Saoi.

"What will happen?" asked Kleena.

"Also very difficult to see with so much potential to end the universe; I am here to witness and help if needed," said Saoi.

"Where has Glic taken the stone?" asked Kleena.

"He is travelling east from Dunluce Castle to Lake Neagh. He's a tricky one and could be anywhere now."

"When will they make the exchange?" asked Kleena.

"It is hard to see through the cloud, with the uncertainty and Balor in the underworld," said Saoi.

"Can you find Glic and take the stone from him?" asked Kleena.

"I can not touch the stone. It may destroy me and erase my consciousness."

"Then kill the one who holds it. Take me, and I will pick it up."

"I can't kill the one who inherits. My force will change the aura of whoever holds it and may implode the universe. I am a witness to the stone, nothing else."

"Kleena! Are you still there?" Brigid called out.

"I'm here," she called back. "Will we meet again?" Kleena asked Saoi.

"It is certain," he answered.

"I have a rope," Brigid said, securing one end to herself and throwing the other over the side of the cliff.

"I look forward to meeting again," said Kleena.

"Under the shelter of each other, people survive," said Saoi.

She turned toward the dark and met a gentle rush of wind. The wind picked her up and whisked her up the cliff, landing next to Brigid.

"What was that? What happened?" asked Brigid.

"I just met with Saoi," Kleena said.

"Is he still down there?" asked Brigid.

"No. He carried me back up the side of the cliff," replied Kleena.

"Did he share any information with you?" asked Brigid.

"He is the spirit of all knowledge!" said Kleena. "He said we are the same, that I am also from the known. Though I have forgotten where I'm from," said Kleena.

"That would help explain why you have suspicions," said Brigid.

"I surely will have to learn more about where I came from," said Kleena.

"Dagda may be able to help you with some of your questions; he can navigate outside our universe. So he may have the knowledge to share," said Brigid.

"Thanks," said Kleena.

"Did Saoi share anything that may help us with our mission?" asked Brigid.

"Yes. He told me an elf named Glic has stolen the stone and is set to deliver it to Balor."

"Oh no! Our darkest suspicion is true. We must find Glic and interrupt the transition. Did he share where this may happen?" said Brigid.

"He mentioned Glic has been tracking southeast from the gateway to Lake Neagh. I believe we can intercept them there. Or, at least, that is where Glic is at the moment. We must get on the move if Balor gets hold of the stone; there is no telling what could happen. He could destroy our universe," Kleena said.

"Do you have a time frame?" asked Brigid.

"No, he could not share this information. He said it's difficult to see, as there is too much uncertainty, and Balor is still in the underworld," said Kleena.

"I am going to Cong to find Runda. You can join us if you wish," said Brigid.

"I feel involved now! I would like to join you. It will be good to see Finn," said Kleena.

With the sun nearly set, Brigid said, "My light-streaming travel may be slow, but shall we go?"

"Yes! Let's do it!"

Kleena took Brigid's hand; both took a deep breath and disappeared into the night.

Chapter 12 Balor

A staple at the peak of a wave
marks the action in response to the intent.
A force in his direction from an unchosen path
lives deep in the psyche of the bloodline.
An entitlement not asked for
is not always the curse that precedes it.
The circumstance is linked to a family
that created a fate because it was the proper choice.
Light is not lost in the dark
but blanketed with unseen transgressions of love and hate.
Plunge into the opposition
as you seek an uncomfortable truth.
The division of life and death
circumnavigates a mysterious partnership that has existed forever.

Morning came fast for Lynx and Dagda as excitement and nervousness clouded their underslept, weary minds.

Lynx had not seen Balor in over two hundred years, and anticipation was growing, especially with the thought that the power-hungry, murderous tyrant was the only thing his kin had become.

Remembering his mother, whom he truly loved as a child, he was abducted by his grandfather at an early age and tossed to the rough sea by Balor in an attempt to kill Lynx, as Balor's death was foreseen to be at the hands of Lynx.

His mother had been suppressed for many years by Balor to prevent the birth of Lynx and his expected death.

Once Balor heard his daughter had a child and was raised secretly, Balor made moves to try to settle his paranoia. He killed Lynx's mother to prevent any more grandchildren.

Balor's insanity grew as his mania drove him to kill all his people and become an all-powerful world leader. His power grew as he consumed all the energy of his people until, so he thought, all his kin were slain.

Now his passion was out of control, and no matter what others did, they couldn't seem to get the upper hand on Balor as he continued to destroy life in his sight. Now he lived stronger. He did not see life with all his kin directly under his control and power, leading to a sad, solitary life. He was so engrossed in misery that destroying all three worlds was starting to seem like the only way out of his mental anguish, without any care or second thought for all life ending because of his destructive ways.

Lynx stood at the edge of the Bush River, looking east toward the sunrise. Today, he found it especially difficult to find happiness in his heart as sadness filled his emotions.

"How are you feeling this morning, Sir Lynx?" Sinsear asked as he very silently snuck up on him.

"Like the last piece of sand in the hourglass," said Lynx, staring at the horizon, not looking down at Sinsear, feeling perplexed. "How do you face your family knowing that you once loved them, and now fate has it that you must release them to the universe?" asked Lynx.

"Emotionally challenging predicament, Sir. I won't claim that I have ever faced such a painful choice. I saw my family die last night, and I sure would do anything to have them back. As you have lost all of your family, I suggest not proceeding with hate in your heart, but rather with your love for your family and knowing you are gaining some justice for them to bring them peace. Know in your heart you will be saving any number of beings from losing their loved ones," said Sinsear.

"You're right; I have hated Balor for so long and felt rage toward him for wanting to come to this moment many years ago. But I fear that I will sense my mom and hesitate for too long when I have my moment.

"The situation will backfire on me, and I will end up with the same fate as the rest of my family if Balor should destroy my body. He may become too powerful even for Dagda to destroy. I am sure glad he is here to face Balor with me. He has been like a father these last two years," said Lynx.

"Dagda is a mighty shoulder to be leaning on; Sir Lynx, I know he is protective of you and will do anything to save you from harm," said Sinsear.

"I also fear putting Dagda in harm's way; many believe in him. If the world loses him, it will be a dark time," said Lynx.

"Dagda can care for himself; he has been around for a long time. I am sure he has a few tricks up his sleeve if needed."

"I feel I should face Balor alone."

"No, Sir, I don't recommend it."

"He will lead you into a death trap."

"We are already in the danger zone. The Pooka is brave and not afraid to die for the cause; we are more likely to be added by the surprise of useless death in Balor's eye. We are committed to serving you, Sir Lynx," said Sinsear. "We have been talking about today and are excited to start the journey that will end Balor's day. We are your scouts. A row has already searched the sky and ground for him."

"You are bold and brave without conviction. We are lucky to have found your clan," said Lynx.

"It is our home. You have come to our camp and entrusted us with an important mission for the underworld; we are ecstatic to bring peace again."

"Lynx, my son, you are an early riser," said Dagda as he approached.

"Good morning, Dagda," Lynx said.

"Sinsear! Always a pleasure."

"Good morning, Dagda," said Sinsear.

"Thanks for the fine welcome as you celebrate the life of your kin; it is a rarity for anyone. I'm sure I feel blessed to have been part of your circle," Dagda said.

"Our circle has just gotten two bigger as we plan to assist you."

"Your dedication to peace is astounding," Dagda said.

"Our desire to free the underworld of Balor's cruel ways has gripped our souls since you arrived to tell us of your plan to kill Balor. Our only focus has become to see you complete your mission safely," said Sinsear.

"Dagda! We should get started travelling," said Lynx.

"You should start your journey south, my friends," Sinsear said. "My kin will have to hound him by now and will track back to find you to give your updates. I smell his foul stench from a hundred kilometres away."

"You and me both, Sinsear," said Lynx.

"I almost sense getting closer to his presence, but I'm not sure if it's good sense or bad."

"You are not alone, Lynx."

"No! I feel as if I am. I have to face him, and all he wants to do is kill me. I'm sure of a delusion of grandeur that I think if he absorbs me, he will be unstoppable," said Lynx.

"I will not let Balor overcome you," said Dagda.

"Dagda, you have been so kind to me even though I have come from a race with a means of taking your land and resources," said Lynx.

"I believe that's an illusion; we are all born on equal ground. It is conditioned in us to think we need to protect our property line or divide ourselves. The walls will come down when we realize we are together to survive and care for one another, losing our greed and a sense of possession. We would have welcomed the Fomorians if they hadn't been so forward in driving us off our land. You were born into this life; it was not your choice, and you should not be condemned for the same. All you can do is move forward knowing you have the support of the masses. Be kind to yourself and brave the noble cause, and you will not be defeated," said Dagda.

"Balor is near Lough Neagh, where the gut of Neagh opens into Lough Beg," said Sinsear.

"I know the area well; we should start our walk while the morning sun is still cool," said Dagda.

"Peace, your Lords, I will see you soon," said Sinsear.

"It's been a time as always, Sinsear; we will see you soon," said Dagda.

Lynx pulled his spear out of the ground and followed Dagda's lead south along the river Bann. Both stared straight ahead, not looking back to give the traditional head nod to Sinsear.

With long strides, they covered a considerable distance in a short time, silent yet focused on the task ahead.

Lynx's mind raced with nervous anticipation of facing Balor. What would commence? What would he say? Would he have the strength and courage to carry on with the mission?

Tired and hungry, Lynx was dizzy and delusional, unlike his ordinary consciousness. He could go days without sleep or food. He started to fall behind a bit as Dagda continued steadily. Lynx became hot and felt a loss of speech as dizzy nausea overcame him.

He walked over to the River to splash the cool water on his face and wake himself up. Blackness shredded his eyesight on the edge of passing out, and he fell to his knees.

Unsure of what was happening, Lynx was having uncontrolled delusions, like his body was telling him something that he could not identify in a clear chronological order.

"I must walk to a location. No, I must sleep. No, stay awake. Where am I? I was with someone; there is something I must do," Lynx muttered to himself as his vision became blurry. He looked around to try to make sense of his surroundings, spotting a spider on his shoulder.

"You must eat." Lynx was sure he heard the spider speak.

"Now I'm sure I'm losing it. What is my purpose here?" he said to himself.

"To eat! You are such a powerful warrior," the spider whispered. "You must eat to keep your strength up."

"Where have you come from, and why do you help me?" asked Lynx.

"I am a friend and want to help remove the pain."

"If you're my friend, why don't I remember you?" said Lynx.

"I may be a stranger, but no less your friend."

Unkindled to everyday reality, Lynx said, "I must eat."

"Yes! Here! You see, delicious mushrooms," the spider said.

"Thank you, my friend. You are most helpful. What would I have done if I didn't meet you?" said Lynx.

"Surely you would die, Sir!" said the spider.

Lynx was dragging a handful of mushrooms. Feeling the urge to eat misguidedly, he shoved a handful in his mouth. Dizzy and wobbling, he chewed and swallowed the mushrooms.

Lynx fell to the ground, but in his mind, he stood up. "I do feel better."

He looked around, trying to remember who he was talking to. Then, he turned to face a young man who looked familiar but was now unknown to Lynx.

"Are you Fomorian?"

"I am."

"How old are you?" asked Lynx.

"Thirteen," said the boy.

"Have we met?" asked Lynx.

"I don't think so," answered the boy.

"Where are we?" asked Lynx.

"Rathlin, of course," said the boy.

"Rathlin? I don't remember coming to the island. I haven't been here in a very long time, and it only brings me memories of heartache," said Lynx.

"It's a peaceful place. You are Fomorian; your family must be here," said the boy.

"We haven't been here in a very long time. Our people used all the resources and had to travel south to find new land to settle."

"Come with me and talk with my elders."

"Lead the way, young man; I am interested in talking with your kin. I thought I was the last of our kind," said Lynx.

"We are two thousand strong and have great support from each other to feed and care for ourselves."

The boy led Lynx up a hill and toward a cave. Lost in a delusional haze, he could not make sense of what was happening. He was certain that his people had died, but sure enough, there was a gathering of Fomorians.

"Come! This way, join us." Said the boy.

"Lugh!" a voice called. "Lugh!" The boy turned to shout back in a snarky tone.

"Yes, Mother, I'm coming," said the boy.

"She's always on my case," he said, turning to run toward his mother.

Lynx was confused that the boy had the same name. Lynx looked ahead at the woman calling, and she bore a resemblance to his mother. The boy ran past her and disappeared into the cave.

"I remember this place. I remember being the boy," Lynx thought.

"Hello, Sir, who are you?" his mother asked. "Where have you travelled from?

"My name is Lynx! I left here many years ago seeking solitude." Lynx answered, sad to be talking to his mother, not sure what was happening.

"Welcome, Lynx. I'm Enyu. Come, feast with us. It's my son's birthday," said Enyu.

Lynx was very uncertain about what was happening, but started walking with his mother, feeling drawn but comfortable with his people.

"What has become of your father?" Lynx asked, confused, as he tried to figure out his bearings in a dream.

"He is well and in the cave, preparing for Lugh's birthday."

Lynx continued to walk, very happy to see his mother, unable to connect the misinformation and confusion, as if it were a dream, just accepting what he saw as a possibility in reality. They made it to the mouth of the cave when Balor walked out. Fear struck Lynx's heart; he stopped, remembering how Balor had already tried to kill him a handful of times. Balor looked like a normal Fomorian.

"What is this?" Lynx thought to himself. "Am I dreaming?"

"This is real," said Balor.

"How do you know what I was thinking?" asked Lynx.

"It's the look on your face," said Balor.

"I have been travelling a long time, and feeling weary," said Lynx.

"Go ahead, join us for the celebration. You are Fomorian." Said Balor, pointing the way, and following closely behind.

"We support each other in difficult times; our people must stick together. I am unifying our efforts. You are home now; there is no need to worry," Balor said.

Lynx was becoming more delusional. "This isn't my home?" he thought to remind himself.

"You are one of us, and this is your home. Come feast with us," said Balor.

As Balor put his hand on Lynx's shoulder, the life in his eyes started to fade. He felt numb and overwhelmed when complying with Balor.

"What are you doing to me?" Lynx asked, feeling powerless.

"You will die and join your family and rise to ultimate power!" Balor said with distain in his voice, as if his power search had no consequences to the lives of others.

"No! No one should think they have all the power. Many people share this sphere of life, and all should hold responsibility and experience peace to find their bliss," said Lynx.

"You can be king; just join us in the cave," Balor said, getting angry.

Lynx weakened, as though venom was running through his veins, when Balor touched him.

"Yes, feel the power; you will submit." All the Fomorians around seemed to fade away as Balor grew to his present self: a massive giant with one eye of light, wearing a helmet with an opening where the light shone through, a trapped light that shouldn't be caged.

Lynx's spear started to glow as Balor squeezed Lynx around the chest. Hands quickly wrapped around and continued to crush the life out of him.

"You will not kill me! I will survive in death to destroy you for killing my family," Lynx said, feeling life come back to him and feeling hope again.

"You have no power or hope of survival over the power I possess; you are delusional if you think you will overcome my stronghold," said Balor.

Lynx suddenly started to have more clarity as he inched closer to death, so he thought.

"I will survive your hatred and bring balance." Lynx reached for his spear, and as he did, the spear started to glow bright white. Lynx, stronger with each breath. The light of the spear blinded Balor, who began screaming out in pain and dropped Lynx to the ground.

Lynx looked up to aim and pushed his spear into Balor's mask to kill him, but as he jolted up in a forward motion, he sat up back at the River Bann, with Dagda sitting over him as he stopped CPR.

"What happened?" asked Lynx.

"You were dead! I found you with a handful of poisonous mushrooms; I have some healing power, but it was too late. Your heart stopped, so I started CPR," said Dagda.

"I'm sorry I walked ahead. I thought I was more of a help ahead of you, watching out for Balor," said Lynx.

"Why did you eat these mushrooms?" asked Dagda.

"I don't know. A spider bit me. I became delusional. I entered a state of death and saw Balor; He tried to kill me."

"Let's get you to safety; Balor must be close, and now he knows we are in proximity.

"Balor likely sensed you, sent word through the spider, and influenced you to eat mushrooms. Then you entered his realm to finish you," said Dagda."How much did you disclose?" asked Dagda.

"Very little, just that I will destroy him for killing my family."

"Good. Let him soak in fear, knowing you are here. He fears your presence because he has been foretold that you will be his demise."

Chapter 13 Ballynoe Stone Circle

Opening the door to a systematic approach
requires planning and practice.
Kitty's opposition threatens his natural talents.
His comforting approach and curious nature
led to an ocean of possibilities,
tuning the mind to listening to the heart
focus on the most logical solutions.
At random times, a piece of the puzzle will approach
before the problem has been presented.
Being in tune with the consciousness of the spirit
enlightens the senses as a foul stench lurks in the shadow.
Mr. Kitty will have to overcome his preconceived fear
and outthink the trickery of his demons.

Mr. Kitty's fur blew steadily back as his eyes watered. The excitement of flying on the back of General Alta was a great sense of adventure. There was no way reading his books would stir this much thrill. It was nearly impossible to have found himself in this predicament, knowing there was no way he would have stumbled upon this place if he hadn't tried.

"How are you doing, Kitty?" Alta asked.

"Shocked and amazed, General. Flight is not natural for cats."

"Well, you're doing fine. Just ease up on the claws a bit."

"Truly sorry, Sir. I didn't realize I gripped so hard," said Mr. Kitty.

"You're fine. We are going to descend now. You may want to hold on for this one."

Alta took a nosedive, followed closely by his two companions, soaring into the forest by Randlestorm, close to Lake Neagh at the edge of the River Maine. Alta guided him into a secret village of the woodland fairies and the home of Athair. Since their arrival was unexpected, the town was quiet, and all fairies were cautious. They disappeared at the sight of unannounced visitors.

Alta floated down to a large rock in front of an impressive Douglas Fir tree. No birds or animals were chattering; it was just the wind through the trees.

Mr. Kitty jumped off Alta's back. He was overjoyed to find his footing on solid ground. Athair and Hazel followed closely behind him.

"Pretty quiet here," said Mr. Kitty.

"We are private fairies, and quick to hide when someone finds their way into the forest," said Hazel.

To Mr. Kitty's surprise, Athair released a magical-sounding whistle, and the village came alive with hundreds of fairies eager to greet their king and princess.

"Peace and love to all of you. It is good to be back in Forest Hide. Although it is sad to say, it will not be long before this perilous time. Our party will stay the night, and before sunrise, we must part ways again. The time of the equinox has arrived, and I must ensure the safety of Ireland so that we can live peacefully beyond the time of Balor."

Cheers arose from the crowd.

"But tonight, I look forward to catching up with you as we mingle and commemorate our return home. Alta and his comrades are pleased to welcome a newcomer to *Tir Na nOg*. Mr. Kitty will spend the evening accompanying Hazel and me on our morning journey; please help him feel at home," said Athair.

Athair stepped down off the rock and started greeting his many admirers. Mr. Kitty was also rushed by many of the woodland fairies, so curious to meet a talking cat; Mr. Kitty was just as big a novelty to the woodland fairies as the fairies were to Kitty. He, in his adventurous glory, felt so at home.

"Are you okay, Kitty?" Hazel asked, concerned that Mr. Kitty was becoming overwhelmed by the attention.

"I'm doing fine, Hazel; very excited to become more acquainted with your kin."

Mr. Kitty especially gained the attention of a young fairy named Aedan, who asked him a hundred questions as if they were ten.

"How did you get here? How did you meet Hazel? How long have you travelled? Where have you travelled to?"

After having met half the village, Mr. Kitty was happy to answer questions and even asked a few questions about his feelings at home by the end of the evening. However, after eating and drinking a lot during the festivities, he became weary and tired of the company. At the same time, Hazel must have been aware of his body language and approached Mr. Kitty.

"I have arranged a bed for you; you must be exhausted?" asked Hazel.

"Much obliged, yes! I am feeling the long day."

"Follow me. I will show you where to sleep tonight to keep out of sight, should curious strangers enter our village."

"Thanks so much, Hazel. Will you wake me in the morning to inform me that we are ready to make our way to Ballynoe?" asked Mr. Kitty.

"Yes. Alta has agreed to help us get to the stone circle safely; I will call you early to have breakfast before we begin our journey," said Hazel.

"Many thanks; I am ready to give in to the sandman and rest my weary body," said Mr. Kitty.

Hazel led Mr. Kitty out of sight of their open gathering space. She led him to a large tree with an opening at the base. There was much room inside to stretch out for a cozy night's sleep.

"This is most gracious; what a great spot to feel safe for the night."

"Good night, Kitty; I will see you bright and early," said Hazel.

"Sleep well, Hazel," Mr. Kitty said, tucking into the tree and settling into the soft moss, drifting into a light sleep.

"Filthy feline; try to kill me, will you? I will take away your happiness as well as your misery. But why does Dagda believe you have a part to play? What is his reason for being here? Should I spare your life or kill you now to prevent your importance?"

Glic came out of the shadows to move closer to Kitty, pulling his knife out of his belt. Since Mr. Kitty was in the tree, Glic could only approach it from one angle. He slowly moved through the forest's darkness, hissing revenge remarks under his breath. As he approached the tree, Mr. Kitty sensed an ill presence, opening his eyes slowly but not moving.

Glic was stealthy in the darkness, but so was Mr.Kitty. Relaxed and calm, Mr. Kitty waited to move before he knew he was safe, but he was too paranoid now.

Glic moved closer to the tree within five feet without any noticeable movement to warn Kitty, when he finally spotted a shadow moving outside the tree.

He let out a low growl, warning whatever creature crept in the night.

"I may not see what my senses can; I can smell your wretched stink, Glic. I recognize your foul odour. I sense your fear and desire for revenge. But you should realize that you tried to kill me and led you to tumble over the cliff edge," Mr. Kitty spoke to the stillness of the night.

"Curious cat has stuck its nose where it doesn't belong. I will kill you to protect the future of peace and power, my lord has set to bestow."

"Balor does not wish for peace; he kills all that should cross his path," said Mr. Kitty.

"Sometimes you need to wipe the slate clean to bring balance," said Glic.

"This is false; the slate does not need to be neutralized, only the enemy causing the disturbance: Balor and his misguided lackey. Where's the stone?"

"What do you know of the stone?" Glic asked snarkily.

"We know you tried to kill Runda under false illusion, like a coward, blindly following deceitful persuasion!" said Mr. Kitty.

"I am not a coward," Glic said as he emerged from the darkness into the moonlight to face the tree, seeing Mr. Kitty's eyes sparkle in the dark.

"You protect your precious ego, not that you tried to kill Runda. You are evil and need to be dealt with by Dagda!"

"Dagda is a fool for not joining Balor's offer to join his efforts for restoring Balance," said Glic.

"You're a fool for believing Balor wishes peace by killing many. You should sacrifice the few to save the many," said Mr. Kitty.

Crack, Crack. Mr. Kitty and Glic turned to see a bright light, and the tree vines shot toward Glic.

Glic grabbed Mr. Kitty's foot while he felt punched in the face, causing him to stumble and fall over. Disoriented with the instinct to survive, he gripped his knife as Athair and two woodland fairy warriors descended toward Mr. Kitty and Glic.

Glic was slippery and stealthy, disappearing into the shadows. The two warrior fairies fled in the direction they saw Glic move.

Athair's staff continued to light up the area.

"Are you okay, Kitty?" asked Athair.

"Yes. Glic did not get close enough before you were here. Thanks for your protection."

"You should feel safe here, Kitty!" said Athair.

"I owe my life to you," said Mr. Kitty.

"You owe me nothing. I am here to protect the peace," replied Athair.

"Glic has the stone! I hope your kin catches him," exclaimed Mr. Kitty.

"He might be slippery, but my warriors are brilliant in tracking," said Athair.

"There are more warriors in the trees here watching over you. I will leave you to sleep and stay here for the night. Knowing you are safe, try to get some rest; we head out at dawn for Ballynoe."

Mr. Kitty slept the most disturbed, as he heard singing in his dreams.

My love is so frail,
Living and longing for peace.

Dark times will prevail,
rising with the ticking time.
Proceeding with light
and goodwill at heart,
will not be caged for the crime.
Fear not; face the dark,
The morning is the truth.
Past, present, future
embark

"Kitty, Kitty!" Hazel said excitedly.

Mr. Kitty awoke with a jump.

"Hazel! Is everything Okay?"

"Yes. How did you sleep? My father told me you had another run-in with Glic."

"Yes, I'm starting not to like him, and I try to find the goodness in everyone."

"He has been dark for a long time, but his true deceitfulness is revealed," said Hazel.

"I just think he is scared and doing what he believes is right for the safety of his future," said Mr. Kitty.

"You are kind without hesitation, Kitty. We should make our way."

Mr. Kitty and Hazel arrived at the governing stone to meet Alta and Athair and have a bite to eat before they took flight.

"Hazel, you were there when Dair came to take me to *Tir na nOg*. Why did he assist me here?"

"Dair and I have been friends for a long time, but sometimes it's a mystery how he knows when to make moves for the well-being of others. He's genuinely one of a kind. He is even more knowledgeable than Dagda, though he is more reserved and enjoys his privacy.

"My father tells me he was among the first to establish a home in *Tir na nOg*. Dagda was enlightened to the birth of the universal knowledge of the early days, born as nature is maintained, giving birth to the trees and spreading the seeds of time. However, consciousness is a tree of knowledge that may have existed before the universal laws," said Hazel.

"I believe he is limited to our three. He saw you at the base of his roots reflected in *Tir a nOg,* even though you were still in your world. When connected to his natural form, he lives in all three worlds simultaneously with the three sisters. He prefers to take the form of Dair, as you know him. But this reflects how he wants you to perceive him."

"That is incredible. Who are the three sisters?" Mr. Kitty asked.

"Eriu, Bandba, and Fodla; they were formative beings here, but it is said they still survive in consciousness; we honour them as if they were still alive. After living for millennia for the island's sovereignty, they gave up their lives for the Island.

"They are understood now as Peace, Love, and Charity. Along with Dair, they are the four corners of our house. They are born and will die with our universe," said Hazel.

"What do you mean they gave their lives?" asked Mr. Kitty.

"As living beings, they realized they were limited, and transformed consciousness into one with nature and the land.

"Stones were erected and charged by them to power the island and ensure that unity survived. Those with good and honest intentions can use that energy to accomplish many impossible feats," said Hazel.

"What impossible feats?" asked Mr. Kitty.

"We are going to visit Banba, one of the three sisters. She is buried under Ballynoe; she will help you travel long distances, unknown for the island's good, and the others. Eriu is the heart of the island. She is believed to be the most powerful and resides near Uisneach Hill at the center of the island. The third is Fada, buried under Dromberg, who also assists with goodwill in travelling for the benefit of the island.

"Good morning, Hazel and Kitty. How did you sleep after meeting with Glic?" asked Athair.

"Unsettled, but I believe I got a few hours. I heard voices in my dreams last night," said Mr.Kitty.

"Voices?" exclaimed Hazel, as if asking a question.

"Yes!" said Mr. Kitty.

They spoke that darkness would prevail unless I proceeded with light and connected to oneness. What does this mean?" asked Mr. Kitty.

"Oneness is a personal journey; once you discover it, it may change how you think and feel," answered Athair.

"It is a realization that you are connected to everything and will never be destroyed. A balance of laws that govern how nature operates. Chaos and calm at the same moment," said Hazel.

"How do I use the light? The voice mentioned that I need to proceed with it, " Mr. Kitty asked.

"The light is inside you and connects you to nature," Athair said.

Two warrior owls landed on the governing stone.

"We should get moving, Athair," said Alta.

"Agreed!"

The three climbed up onto the owl. The crowd of woodland fairies gathered, hushed as they looked upon their king and princess. "Peace to you; we shall return with good news. Be safe," said Athair.

The silence remained as they took to the air. Alta and his two partners powered their way up, skimming the tops of the trees and heading east. Mr. Kitty is overjoyed at his chance to fly on the back of Alta.

Mr. Kitty was so happy to have this view of the countryside. Tuning into all his senses, he felt at peace with his experience. It didn't seem long before they descended to an open field, where he could see a stone circle take shape as they flew closer.

Alta landed so gracefully, and Mr. Kitty jumped down.

"Welcome to Ballynoe. This is a special place where you will start to see the magic surrounding you in this thin spot," Alta said to Mr. Kitty.

"Peace, my friends," Athiair said to Alta.

"We shall meet again soon," Alta said as he took flight.

"What did he mean, a thin spot?" asked Mr. Kitty.

"A thin spot is a power spot. It can be a challenge to travel between worlds in just any location on the island, but a thin spot refers to a place that connects worlds and other dimensions. It is almost like the veil that separates worlds is removed," said Athair.

"Amazing!" said Mr. Kitty.

"Hazel, you mentioned one of the three sisters is buried here."

"Yes, Banba rests in the middle of the circle."

"How do we use this spot?" asked Mr. Kitty.

"Come with me, open your heart, be at peace; you will likely have no problems here. Think of Cong and your desire to help Runda as we enter the centre. You shall be untraceable if Glic is still tracking us," said Hazel.

"Should we find Glic to lure him in and see what he did with the stone?" asked Mr. Kitty.

"No, we should carry on our mission by the spirit circle and find Runda to save his life. Glic will try to find a way to the underworld to give Balor the stone, and Lynx and Dagda will already be close to Balor," said Athair.

"Okay! Let's do this," Mr. Kitty said.

The three stepped into the circle, slowly walking closer to the centre, and then disappeared like smoke in the wind.

Chapter 14 Runda

Putting luck in a case
is putting wind in a cage.
It is not held and fully embraced until it's time to let go.
Saving a life requires a team approach.
Runda has given his breath to Aurora,
a division most necessary to overcome life versus death.
The way of the Leprechaun is to live
at the crest of this natural partnership.
The treasure is in the emotional feeling of caring and sharing.
Far more will be saved in this realm.
Mr. Kitty is the light, the breath, and the body
Cornerstones for the building blocks of success
in finding Runda and saving his life.

Padraig, a patron of Ireland. Honoured in his chosen path, to bring word to the land. Lives a quiet life and holds many secrets of the spirit. A Saint to the people and a bringer of hope. His strong will enables him to overcome adversity, trying to mend a dispute with a helping hand and a blessing.

Along with his friend and witness to the word, Shannon, kneels at the bedside. Wearing the most elegant beige lace dress, her long, dark hair was adorned with flowers that held it back, revealing her beautiful, fair skin. However, the tear in the corner of her eye sparkled as it fell onto Rundas' hand.

The priest's house is on the other side of the river that runs through Cong. Runda is no more than seventy-two centimetres tall and has a long beard. He is usually a jolly fellow, well-fed and drunk on life, with rosy cheeks. Now, he lay pale, grey and motionless.

"I'm losing him; Shannon, pass me the towels. The wound is infected, and I think he is bleeding internally. I must cut the sutures to relieve the pressure," said Padraig.

"Padraig," Shannon said softly. "I fear we are losing him; his pulse is getting weaker and more thready."

Padraig opened the wound to Runda's abdomen, and a large amount of purulent drainage and fresh blood poured out of the wound.

They cleaned and dressed the wound as thoroughly as possible.

"What shall we do?" Shannon said, feeling at a loss, with having a personal battle to prepare herself for the death of her friend. "We will need nothing short of a miracle to save his soul at this point," Padraig said.

They sat over Runda. Another tear fell from Shannon's eye as she was about to lose one of her best friends, while Padraig prayed.

Dear Heaven, we need you,
Your presence will surround us, help Runda, or guide him home.
He has carried the spirit stone for a long time
and deserves the peace you provide.
Please carry him over the rainbow bridge
to a place of painlessness and peace with no needs
To be on the move, no more protecting the treasure
that you have entrusted to him,
For one is the kingdom
forever and ever.

"Maewyn, are you here?" Brigid called from outside the priest's house.

"Padraig, it's Brigid," she said as she opened the door, seeing Runda lying on the bed with her old friend hovering over, trying to save his life. Sadness embraced her as she felt the pain of the island gripping her emotions.

"Oh, Brigid, I am so glad you are here," said Padraig. He stood up to give her a warm embrace.

"Runda is dying," said Shannon. "Are you able to help?"

"Maybe," Brigid answered.

"This is Kleena; she is here to assist me. We will do our best to save him."

"My heavens, Kleena; I have heard tales of you bringing the foreshadowing of death. Do you bring the same news for our friend's future?" asked Padraig.

"I hope not, Padraig."

They moved closer to the bed and saw Runda lying motionless on the bed. "Kleena, we should join hands and stand on either side of the bed," said Brigid.

"Can I do anything to help?" asked Padraig.

"Yes. We will try the power of three," said Brigid.

"We may have the power to heal and clear this infection with your assistance."

Kleena, Brigid, and Padraig joined hands.

Kleena and the power of the known, Padraig with the power of the spirit, and Brigid with the power of the knowledge of the elements circle Runda, as Brigid prays:

With the assistance of the
Earth, wind, fire, water, and spirit.
We entrust you to heal our friend Runda, clear his aura of death,
breathe life back into his body,
fight the infection, and
Heal his wounds.

The three stood over him, joining hands as the light dimly glowed in the centre and appeared to surround Runda. Slowly, the redness left his wound, and colour returned to his face.

Shannon removed the towels from Runda's abdomen to see it healing before her eyes. But Runda did not wake up. Shannon kept close to him, helpless, trying to do whatever she could. She put three fingers on the inside of his wrist along his thumb.

"His pulse is fading," Shannon said as Brigid, Kleena, and Padraig emerged from their trance.

"Incredible though, his wound is gone," said Padraig in amazement at what he just experienced. Looking up at Brigid and Kleena with a new respect for them.

"I fear we may be too late," said Brigid, disheartened.

"I lost the pulse," Shannon said softly as she started to cry.

"Please do something, Brigid?" Kleena said as her fears came to the surface. If this were happening, then what she had foreseen would also be true.

Kleena kneeled beside the bed to hold Runda's hand, "I remember seeing this moment. I'm sorry to say my affirmation has come true. What would turn the light to darkness?" Kleena said with concern.

"Runda was just an obstacle in their way. He is so much better than to end like this," Shannon cried out in pain and love at the loss of her friend. "Please, wake up, Runda!"

Brigid, heartbroken, said, "I have the power to heal, but not bring back to life. That truly would be a miracle."

Silence fell over the room as they mourned the death of a legend, knowing that a small part of life's lucky magic had departed from this world, and life would never be the same.

A cool breeze and a foggy mist, with hints of green and gold, filled the priest's house and began to take shape at the end of the bed.

"Athair, Hazel, and Kitty, now have you come to us?" Brigid amazed at

"Glic was following us, so we travelled to Ballynoe with the power of Banba to bring us to Runda," said Athair.

"Are we too late? Has Runda died?" asked Mr. Kitty.

"Yes," answered Kleena.

Mr. Kitty tucked himself behind Brigid at the sight of Kleena; the last time he had seen her, she was a ghost bringing the news of Runda's death.

"It's okay, Kitty; this is Kleena. She means you no harm, and this is Padraig and Shannon. They are priests sharing the word of the spirit," said Brigid.

"Brigid, what shall we do? You have the power of the druid to heal," said Athair.

"Yes, heal, but not bring back life. We need a lot more than I can offer," she answered. Then Brigid brightened up with excitement, as a solution was right before her eyes.

"We can use the power of five; Kitty is a pure spirit and lives a mortal life. Please, Kitty, sit on Runda. We shall use his innocence, and share the breath of life back into Runda with the elements of: Earth, Athair; Air, Padraig; Fire, Brigid; And water, Kleena. The spirit at the centre with Kitty, we may have a chance to save his life," said Brigid, feeling encouraged.

Mr. Kitty hopped on the bed and sat on Runda's stomach.

"Come on, everyone, join hands around Kitty and Runda," Brigid said, reaching out to join hands with the others as she said aloud.

"Power of the spirit,
Join us now
Earth, Fire, Water, Wind, Spirit
Breath of Life
Infinity of Death
Worlds Above and Below
Restore the youth
The life of our brother Runda"

Smoke filled the circle in a rainbow of colours. It was sucked into Mr. Kitty's lungs as he breathed. The four around Runda had their eyes closed, while Shannon and Hazel watched in amazement as Mr. Kitty's aura glowed, moved down to his paws, and entered Runda's chest, making his aura shine. They appeared as if surrounded by water. Mr. Kitty's fur flowed, and Runda's beard flowed as well.

The light and mist settled into Runda as stillness overcame the room.

"Why is there a kitty sitting on my belly?" Runda said as they all cried in amazement.

"You're alive!" Shannon called as she ran over to the bed to hug Runda, swinging him around like a teddy bear.

"Easy, easy, my love," he cried. "Where have all you fine people come from? Padraig, what is happening? Where is my stab wound?"

"They came to your aid to bring you from the dead!" said Padraig.

"Well, that's a story I don't hear daily. Glic has taken the spirit stone. I am not sure how he tracked me down," said Runda.

"He escaped us last night. Kitty had a run-in with him. The woodland fairies are trying to track him," said Athair.

"He will likely be trying to get to the underworld to give the stone to Balor," said Brigid.

"My heavens, Brigid and Athair. I'm sure I have failed to get the attention of such royalty," said Runda.

"You haven't failed," Brigid said. "We have called a meeting of the spirit circle, which is brought together to find you and the stone. Dagda and Danu head the circle."

"I am truly blessed to have such friends here. Thank you from one end of the rainbow to another. I may have lost my treasure, but you gave me the best gifts: love and friendship," said Runda.

"Don't worry about the stone, Runda; you must rest. You have been through a lot over the last few days, and have died," said Athair.

"I most certainly do not feel unwell. I have never felt so good in my life: recharged and eager to find that greedy, nothing Glic and bring him what he has coming. A most welcome ending to his life?" said Runda.

"Rest, my friend," said Padraig. "We will have time to regroup and develop a strategy to find Glic, or the next best step."

"I know most of you, but I haven't met two of you before," said Runda.

"I'm Kleena."

"Are you? I know you. I truly must have died if you are here; I heard of your legend."

"I did foresee your death and felt drawn to be here to save you when Brigid found me down. This gives me hope for what can be accomplished when given a foreshadowing from the known," said Kleena.

"And who brought this cat?" asked Runda.

"I'm Kit Cat, but you can call me Kitty."

"My lucky charms, what a mystery to have brought a talking cat to my service."

"It's a great honour to meet you," said Kitty.

"Surely the honour is mine; you have saved my life," Runda said.

"Kitty is the key to your survival; he has the favour of the universe. His innocence is the spirit you needed, and with the power of five, we brought the spark back to you," said Brigid.

"It sounds like this gathering is all by chance," said Runda.

"The language and mystery of the spirit continue to mystify me every day," said Padraig.

"The next word that spreads will be when St. Patrick raises the dead," Shannon giggled.

"It's a group effort; with the help of friends, any obstacle will be overcome," said Padraig.

"Well, I am certainly happy you all were here," said Runda.

"What has become of Balor? Do we know where he is and what he is doing?" asked Runda.

"Lynx and Dagda are tracking him in the underworld. He has been trying to break through the gateway. Though Finn has been wearing himself thin trying to keep Balor from entering *Tir na nOg*," said Brigid.

"It's good. They are on their way to find him. Glic said I would wish I were dead once Balor got the stone," Runda continued.

"He plans on ruling over all three worlds and killing all who get in the way, starting with Lynx. Glic thinks it is time to side with Balor to save my future. But I said I would cross the rainbow bridge before giving allegiance to Balor.

"He believes that once he kills Lynx, he will be powerful enough to walk through all three worlds at once. While turning the world to darkness so that he can use our universe like his personal vessel, potentially destroying other universes with his sight set on the luminous beings to dim their light, to become an all-powerful God," said Runda.

"His delusions match paranoia," said Brigid.

"How do you know this?" asked Padraig.

"I have been keeping a silent eye on him myself, feeling that I have been holding the stone for so long and Balor has been gaining power, so I thought I should keep a close eye on my enemy. He talks to himself out loud when he doesn't see anyone around him. His distorted illusion of the future is getting worse," said Runda.

"Will the stone give him this power he seeks?" asked Mr. Kitty.

"No! The stone is not meant to be used for the power it possesses. It balances, endlessly trying to bring balance to energy. Suppose one tried to use the stone to destroy the natural energy flow. In that case, there'd be a tsunami of energy, likely to kill the one who holds it and possibly implode our universe, bringing the unknown to complete resolution."

Runda said the stone was not an energy source, but a center of gravity for the three-dimensional universe.

"Have you picked up any info about his weakness?" Mr. Kitty asked.

"Legend tells that his grandson, the last of the Fomorians, will be the one who takes him down. Balor is very fearful that this will come to fruition. He fears Lynx the most and continues trying to kill him, fearing his demise. So Lynx needs our protection, because he may be our only hope against him. Protecting the stone from getting into his ill-conceived hands will be most important," said Athair.

"So I must attract Glic's attention to distract him so we can get the stone," said Mr. Kitty.

"We can't put you in that position," said Brigid.

"He wants to kill me; I can pull him out of the shadows," said Mr. Kitty.

"I think this may be a way," said Hazel. "We can protect him; I will never leave his side. It is dangerous. But getting the stone to keep it safe can save the universe."

"You're brave, Kitty. I, too, will be by your side," said Athair.

Suddenly, Kleena went pale grey.

"Are you okay, Kleena?" asked Brigid.

She did not answer. "She's in a trance," said Athair.

"Should we try to wake her?" asked Padraig.

"No, don't disrupt her," said Brigid. "She is tapped into the known. You could trap her forever, or kill yourself in the process."

Kleena slowly lifted off the floor, appearing dark, with a shadowy light floating in the water.

Mhor bais
much death on the horizon, the bridge between lands,
The gap between the world
A battle of light and dark
destroying all in its path
Many marrows find peace in the depths
trying to save our existence
Elves, Humans, Giants, Druids, Fairies
We all need to find common ground
to make it to Dawn.
If Kitty turns to stone,
All will be united in peace.

Kleena slowly settled back to her feet, and colour returned to her face. Everyone in the room remained silent as they looked at Kleena.

"You were bringing a message from the known," said Brigid.

"I have no control over it; what did I say?'

"You said there will be a battle at the gateway, where death awaits all races unless we work together against Balor," said Padraig.

"You also mentioned something about Kitty turning to stone and being united in peace. Is that death peace or life peace?" asked Brigid.

"We should all make our way to the gateway with Finn, for he will need our help," said Mr. Kitty.

"Balor is at the gateway; Glic will also be heading back since he lost track of Kitty," said Hazel.

"We should go back to Dunluce with Runda to meet with Danu to develop a plan," said Athair.

"It will be best to get back tonight, because the message was that the Battle will be before Dawn, so we have a timeline," said Padraig.

"You do not have to put yourself in harm's way, Padraig," said Brigid.

"I am in harm's way, and sitting back to watch things unfold is not in my nature. I feel dedicated to the island and the spirit," said Padraig.

"You should remain here, Shannon; the people need support now."

"If you wish, I will stay here and pray for your speedy, safe return."

"It's done, then; we shall make a speedy journey to Dunluce," said Brigid.

Chapter 15 Lir to Ri

The solstice of the world turns into a vortex
as chaos leads the weary travellers to the surface.
A beauty of fiery destruction built the land,
creating the hill that connects the land and sea.
Death gives birth as the circle of life endures change.
From chaos comes predictability.
Overcoming the evil eye that brings havoc
is deciphering its sophistry,
as it promises heaven when it gives hell.
The strength of the opposition, who sees the truth,
is not lost in deceit but is in the hope of survival.
A shadowy fear could be familiar love.

Lir stood on the shore early in the morning. The sun lit up the heavens, creating a fiery crimson horizon. The distance from the underworld to heaven shifted slightly in his direction, as thoughts of a clouded future smothered his mind.

"Am I losing my mind, or is midnight coming quicker than I am prepared for? I have always seen the possible futures; neither can I see nor predict what will become of the fog before me," Lir thought to himself.

"These old bones have ruled the land and sea for too long. Is it my future that is uncertain rather than the future of Ireland? How is it that I can't see past the equinox? I will regain strength and insight soon."

Lir raised his hands in the air.

"Life from water, wisdom from within," he said, and from the still shore, a mist rose; the rough seas shaped like horses rushed out of the water to meet him.

"Hello, friend; we must find Ri."

Lir reached up to touch the neck of one of the four horses formed from the water. Then Lir saw the sea, and the Merrows, Ri and Kara gathered with hundreds of loyal followers.

The land and sea had come to misunderstand each other, and with differences came stereotypes and misinformation that drove a wedge between the souls living in their respective places.

The kingdom of Ri and his merrow court remained dedicated to the peace and love between land and sea. A few judgmental merrows had accepted the division and made themselves unseen from Balor.

There was a misplaced perception that the land folk deserved what they had coming with Balor. They didn't see how it would affect the weather, so they made themselves scarce.

"I must get to them; time to stem the tide, old friend."

He walked into the ocean, like walking into that from which he came.

He was completely submerged. The current whisked him away, and the four seahorses escorted him into the depths toward the morrow court, which lay west of the gateway.

The tide was in Lir's favour as they sped toward the merrows, but an uneasy feeling that he couldn't shake had gripped his soul, flushing visions of dark shadow in the belly of the ocean floor.

He was moving toward the gateway. Lir could not place the darkness he was sensing, fearing that maybe Balor had been working on his strength to push through.

He combed the ocean floor with his eyes as he whisked by. He knew what he was feeling, and it was not Balor in the darkness. His thoughts brought attention to his adverse experience at the planet's birth.

Samwin was showing signs of rising her fiery head. She was a monster and a serpent to some, and though misunderstood by most, she had coerced herself into hiding for over two thousand years. People feared her and imagined her being chased away, so she allowed them to believe the same. She was a peaceful being who should be celebrated, but hid with free will to give the people a sense of safety.

Creating a balance in the ecosystem with Lir, Water, and Fire gave rise to and shaped the land and the atmosphere. She may have been curious about the movement at the giant's gateway and felt the threat to the ecosystem.

She balanced the three dimensions, helping despite being chased away under the sea. But now she was finding her way back from the earth's core.

Having lived immortal to the time restraints that restricted them all, she was apathetic to the outcome, willing to accept her demise if it was so. Now, a threat at the chosen hands of a few, she felt her energy drain.

Lir slowly came closer to the gateway. Sand appeared to be kicking up, creating a dust cloud.

"*Dia dhuit*, Sam," Lir said to the sandy cloud.

"Good to see you well," Samwin said as the dust took the form of a young woman.

"I have not heard tell of you in a millennium. People don't even mention your name much," said Lir.

"Why have you come looking for me?" asked Samwin.

"I sensed your activity; I thought maybe Balor was getting closer," said Lir.

"He is!" said Samwin. "And it won't be long before he makes it to *Tir na nOg*!"

"You should find help if you wish to defeat Balor. With Unity comes strength," said Samwin.

"Will you not help? Balor threatens you; it is you he wishes to overthrow."

"I've existed for too long, after what seems like endless time, and I've been chased to the basement of my house. The people I helped raise have denied me and turned me into a demon when I gave them life. If today shall bless me, I shall welcome the known with all my heart," said Samwin.

"The people that live and celebrate your name shall die," said Lir.

"I did not cause this destruction and shall not interfere. I am tired," Samwin said.

"You have been hidden away so long, feeling defeated, that you are becoming the very thing you were running from. Mother, if you leave them to die, I know your conscience that lives on will find regret," said Lir.

"I'm absolved of the action. I did not bring this movement; I will dissolve into the calmness of dark matter, as nothingness, feeling free from the abuse with which beings have been treating me," said Samwin.

"You are honoured here; you are not a monster. Yes, you deserve to be treated better. But I will fight. I know you will not give up on our people; they have good that is suppressed. They will change for the better; they just need you to remind them of the importance of life." Lir continued, "Please do not abandon us now in our time of uncertainty and vulnerability."

"I am awake now and will know what is happening for you; I will consider my presence to protect our children," said Samwin.

"Keep in touch, Samwin. I missed you; we used to be so close. I hope we will be again. Do not hide for so long."

"You're kind, Lir. When you are at odds and under pressure, it is sometimes best to remain neutral, allowing the current to flow naturally. Before you proceed, know that Balor will rise at dawn," Samwin said as she put her hands together as though in prayer, gave the nod as she faded to dust and sand floating in the water, and dispersed.

"Peace be with you," he spoke to the dust and smoke. "Make haste, and set a course to Ri."

Without looking like any effort was made on behalf of the horses, they were speeding toward the court of the marrow king.

Ri was a young and mighty king of the marrows, with fifteen feet of silver and gold armour to fit his broad shoulders, covering his torso. He was stealthy in the water, unafraid of anything, even if Balor pushed through the coulombs. Ri would not hesitate to be the first to meet him and his stone-cold stare.

"My fellow merrow, we rule the sea, so we have the privilege to protect the shore. Today, we face our greatest challenge: a monster in the state to rule all. His greatest strength shall be the cause of his downfall. He is clouded in his delusion that he has any power to overcome the power of unity in the masses for the peace and goodwill of the island.

"We shall band together, making current in the direction of the gateway and attempting to end this poisonous hold on *Tir na nOg*. He may walk the land, but he has to get through us," said Ri.

Lir arrived at the court, entering from behind a stone altar as Ri addressed the marrows.

Kara floated down to meet Lir, dressed in a knightly royal suit of armour. A pale blue aurora seems to radiate out of her.

"Lir!" Kara said softly as she approached.

"Princess Kara, it's been too long. How are you?" asked Lir.

"We are well. Balor pushes through the columns while we prepare for the day, and we can sense he has been making headway."

"Yes, I must speak to your father."

Cheers continued as Ri rose from the altar. Looking down at Kara and Lir, with one flick of his fin, he glided down to meet Lir.

Both Lir and Ri smiled happily to see each other.

"Ahoy, my old friend," said Lir.

"So much for the small talk. It's great to have you here. What warning do you see?" asked Ri.

"Balor will rise at dawn," said Lir.

"We sensed he was getting close, but there was no activity. I figured he ran out of steam and took a rest," said Ri.

"I'm not sure Balor rests anymore," said Lir.

"He operates more like a machine than a Fomorian."

"Even a machine will break down." Ri continued, "The marrows are prepared to fight at the gate at Dawn. We have been anticipating this day."

"You are fearless, Ri. I will accompany the merrow king to the depths of the underworld for freedom from this fear," said Lir.

"It is an honour to fight with you; we shall claim victory over Balor this day. Kara, you must stay behind, for I fear for your safety! You are a princess; if I fall, you must take my place," Ri said.

"You must not take the front line either. We need you, too. Balor is strong and ruthless, and will not turn his eye away to save the king of the merrow," said Kara.

"I am not just king today; I am the strongest of the merrow and a force for Balor to overcome. Come with me, Lir, to address the news of Balor to the court," said Ri.

The three glided up to the altar and, through the large arches, faced the merrow warriors.

"My brothers and sisters, please welcome Lir," Ri said.

Cheers shrieked through the water.

"We are blessed and honoured to have him here with the marrows during these dark times. Lir brings news of Balor," said Ri.

Silence overcame the crowd.

"It is predicted that Balor will return to the gate and will push through to *Tir na nOg* at Dawn," said Ri.

Faint chatter could be heard as the marrows talked amongst themselves. Lir spoke again:

"The land and sea give the illusion of being separate. We know that what affects one will affect the other; Balor looks to push into our world, take control over and rule the land, or even destroy everything you take for granted.

"We are all aware that the spirit stone is missing. If Balor gains control of the stone, he will potentially harm himself and may implode the universe, neutralizing all three worlds we have come to know and love.

Merrows are a solid force to be reckoned with. We shall not give up easily. We are living and dying with love on our side. Strength in love has no competition and shall endure all that tries to overcome our stronghold.

We kept the peace by being passive and quiet, but tonight, we will show Balor what we can do when we move together, loudly and persistently.

If we don't end his misery at dawn, we shall drive him back to the underworld," said Lir

Yells and cheers were so loud, it was as if Balor had already been defeated. Ri spoke as Kara stood next to her father.

"We are many, yet we are one; we have trained hard and anticipated this day. Let's go forth with no fear in our hearts. Balor may take our breath, but he does not win our light."

At that moment, Kara's necklace started to glow. She looked down and held her pendant. She looked over at her father, concerned by the pendant's glow.

"What is it, Kara?" said Ri.

"It's Kitty. The spirit circle has called him to help find the spirit stone. I gave him my twin pendant so he could contact me if he found himself in danger and needed the merrows' assistance. He calls from the gateway."

Ri raised his hands to signal the merrows' attention, and silence quickly overcame him.

"The time has come. The spirit circle calls us with distress calls from the gateway. Balor shall meet the wrath of the merrows."

The army of merrows quickly turned northeast, making waves toward the gateway. Ri, Kara, and Lir followed closely.

Chapter 16 Grange Stone Circle

Fields in a silent mist, natural to its thinness
The soul opens to the oneness, where time seems infinite
Spring wakes the luminous birth, a trickle of the quickening
Life starts a new cycle, leading to the waking
Summer warms the heart and rids it of its hunger
Renew the Spirit to days of Nature's blossom.
Fall predicts our decline.
Becoming vulnerable to nature.
Challenging stamina at the beginning of the end.
Power, with mind and heart, needs to work together.
Winter's failing health will subdue our ability to carry on in light of
youth.
Peace and acceptance are our strongest allies
To open the solar balance and inevitable guidance into the
evening sun.

Dusk had fallen over the land, and an eerie stillness foretold the coming storm. Dair and Danu had peace in their hearts, though uneasiness clouded the island.

Fear had left their hearts to the oneness in the spirit of nature, which comforted them in times of trial.

They departed from Dunluce and the spirit circle and travelled south, searching for luminous beings at Grange Stone Circle. They were built and charged by the *Tuatha DE Danann*. The *Aos Si*, Danu's people, arrived before the Fomorians arrived in the North.

"Too long have we lived the same story, Dair," said Danu.

"This equinox will end the influence of old governing ways."

"I sense change, but I'm unsure if it is the end of Balor or us."

"Maybe it is time to accept our fate and slowly fade to the west," said Danu. "Balor is strong, and getting the stone has been a worry amongst the *Aos Si*. They speak of Balor returning to *Tir na nOg*, killing the one with the stone and making it his own."

"How would *Aos Si* have such insight?" asked Dair.

"Their nature allows them to live three days ahead and behind. The past and future are their present. The luminous ones are of the known, and this existence gives them their way of taking on the shape that you observe them in. It is rare to see them in proper form," said Danu.

"You've been in contact? When?" asked Dair.

"Three days ago."

"They will know the future; if they have today, we will know what the future may bring."

"They must give us insight!"

"This is why we came to the Grange stone circle. They will be coming to exit *Tir na nOg*," said Danu.

"Tricky!" said Dair.

"The original stone circle is our most-used passage," said Danu. "They can be fast, so you don't see them."

"So why would they talk with us?" asked Dair.

"I'm not sure they will, but I have called upon them to shed light. The last time they were here, they left the island and the people behind, vulnerable to the elements and those who overstayed their welcome. I am a descendant of the luminous ones. I chose to face the Ice Age with Earth and settle in Ireland. They have not communicated with me and my kin, leaving us to succumb to life's wear. Since they left, I felt it was a choice to be silent," said Danu

"Why make contact now?" asked Dair.

"They warned of Balor, knowing we have formed a spirit circle seeking answers and aiming to save the world from mass delusion and paranoia. Running the world with this combination is lousy energy; thinking they should rule the world will only be suitable for some.

"Balor's rise to power will also indirectly affect the ecosystem. He gained their interest; they needed to follow what was happening," said Danu

"Hard times need the light to shine?" Dair said.

"*Aos Si* looked at us from the tower of white; no man or earthly being shall navigate that mountain and sea—the apex. Where only the light of truth shall pass the threshold, they now focus on the gate and the threat of the mighty wind that stalks their security," said Danu.

"Who comes this way to disturb my peace?" a voice came from the brush.

Dair and Danu look toward the voice coming from the Hawthorn tree.

"Cat got your tongue, strangers from the north, what ill fortune do you bring my way?"

"We don't mean to disturb you or bring ill fortune," said Danu.

"Please leave," the voice said. "You have no business here."

"I am Danu, and this is Dair. We are ambassadors to Ireland. We only wish you peace, and we will be on our way soon. Who are you? May I ask?" said Danu.

"You may, but I don't have to answer," he said.

"Will you show yourself?" asked Dair.

A stocky-looking pirate troll, no taller than two feet, emerged from the tree.

"I should warn you that Grange has not been used for travel in millennia, so I made this place my home. It seems out of the way enough since I prefer my own company. Now, strange things are happening here; be gone with you," he spoke.

"What's your name?" asked Dair.

"George. Now, I wish to be left alone."

"Have you seen activity in the circle?" asked Dair

"Not in three days when a wolf and bear passed through," said George/

Dair and Danu look at each other with slight smiles.

"What are you smiling at?"

"Inside joke."

"What do you know of a wolf and bear travelling together?" asked George.

"As far as we know, it is just a bear and wolf, our concerned little friend," said Dair.

"I know you bring an ill fortune with you. What should I read from this riddle when a bear and wolf return, approaching with my dead grandmother, who passed away many years ago?" said George.

Dair and Danu only recognized what George saw once they turned around. Danu did not see a bear, wolf, or troll. He saw a large Red Emperor Deer, a beautiful fairy glowing with a hint of the white aura surrounding her, and an earthly-looking fairy with white eyes.

Dair saw three pure white, oval orbs with thousands of snowflake lights moving around them.

The pirate troll fled to the hawthorn tree, fearing the bear, wolf, and dead grandmother, while Danu and Dair intercepted the three *Aos Si.*

"Before you part from this world, please share knowledge to enlighten our path," spoke Dair.

"We know of tomorrow," said the Aos Si.

"Yes, but now you are three days closer and can envision the future even further. What new wisdom will you share with us? " Danu asked.

"Thunder from invisible clouds will shake the vacuum of the sphere, sending ripples through the cosmos from the heart as the east wind meets the west wind at the centre of the island. The purity of the innocent shall turn to stone as experience has been gained, and that same innocence shall be given up.

Kings to dust and servants to crest upon the horizon of that which the wind is born.

The cold of ruin will illuminate the wise and release the ignorant; three worlds will feel the impulse of death." Said the Aos Si.

"Whose death, how many?" asked Danu.

"Disclosure of this information will change the outcome to what is in motion."

"Why do you leave now? How much destruction is coming?"

"We leave because we do not influence what is happening."

"Is it Balor that dies?" asked Danu.

"Balor will survive."

"Why won't you help us? Balor's light of death is intense. You will feel the effects of his wrath," said Dair.

"The *Aos Si* can not help or prevent that which is happening. We are indifferent. Your universe evolves when the stone elements meet the hand of its final resting spot."

"What should we do next?" asked Danu.

"You will go to the gateway, save Mr. Kitty. He is on the shoreline, vulnerable and endangered by the one named Glic.

"Balor will breach the gateway, and a battle will commence. Ireland will band together to save the island from a death-riddled dictatorship living in fear."

"Is there something we can do for the best possible outcome?" Dair said.

The beautiful Aos Si spoke to Danu:

"Danu will come with us and join the night, ascending back to the known. You have accomplished much for the earth and universe, earning an ascension back to where you came from."

"I can't leave now; I am committed to the people here. If I die, I die with Ireland," said Danu.

"Brigid will carry on your work."

"She and Dagda can watch over and care for the land."

"I will stay and see this through," said Danu.

"Very well. We leave you now. Living in fear will impede the light of love in your heart. Embrace unconditional empathy for your kin. In times of change, you must abolish hate and greed, replacing them with tenderness and compassion for all life,`` said *Aos Si.*

The short, stocky troll dropped out of the hawthorn tree, saying, "Grandmother, is that you? What sorcery has brought you back to bring omen of death?"

The three *Aos Si* did not respond to this question but floated into the stone circle, dissolving into light particles and disappearing.

"Where is she going? Grandmother?" said George.

Distorted by this experience, he turned his confused thoughts toward Danu and Dair.

"You bring her back. What have you done with her?" said George.

"We haven't done anything with her. Your grandmother was not here; that was *Aos Si*. The vision you saw is a reflection of you. The light passed through you to bring light to the vision," said Danu.

"They can bring your inner artifacts to the surface," said Dair.

"Lies! *Aos Si* is a fable," spoke George. "This is a bad omen; you two are supporters of Balor."

"I'm sad the vision of your grandmother has disturbed you; instead, find peace and see this vision as a blessing and a sign of hope," said Dair.

"Nothing good will come from the dead rising," George said. "You will surely get what you have coming by associating yourself with dark magic."

He was gone just as quickly as the short, stocky troll came into their lives.

"Time to move. The day has started, so we should get to Kitty," said Danu.

"Agreed," Dair spoke as they both turned north and disappeared into the light.

Chapter 17 Balor to the Gateway

Once there were many, now they become one.
Believing that one is the nature
Which laws will prevail.
It's one to subdue now conquers the many.
Balor leads the many to follow blindly
At the loss of self and unknowing;
People grew significantly in their resistance.
Lynx has the freedom of choice;
and lacks careful discipline.
The division will benefit, as the nature of the fellowship
Indoctrinates the many in harmony and peace.
The individual with enlightenment
has the responsibility to find the strength to do what's right.

Dagda and Lynx sat at the side of Lough Beg, north of Lough Neagh. They were drained of energy for the long, hot day, walking south, anticipating Balor of the evil way. Lynx nearly faced his death in the light of Balor, who sought to eliminate him, tired and confused. He knew they were close and must find the strength to face what he had come to destroy.

"How are you doing?" asked Dagda.

"Tired, Eagna. How do I face Balor? What do I do?" asked Lynx.

"Anticipating an inevitable moment can drive your emotions and thoughts crazy. It's best to face the situation as if you know what to say and do it confidently. Don't overthink before you submerge in the moment," said Dagda.

"People think they know me better than I know myself. This weight they have on me is overbearing and intimidating. I feel like myself because I am who I am. However, they gave me a responsibility that I hadn't asked for. I know deep down it is me; it's the path I face. I would have taken on the challenge regardless. But this pressure is unwanted.

"I feel anguish toward the people for having so much trust in me. It's likely fake trust; they fear taking on the responsibility themselves," said Lynx.

"It's not fake trust; you are a strong warrior and mentor to them. They look up to you. You can help alleviate a fear that has haunted people for a long time. They just want to rid the day of living in a sacred, sorrowful way.

"Balor can affect them in a way that you are resistant to. You are not easily swayed and will not die at the eye of Balor as quickly. You're Fomorian! Yes, they see this and put added pressure on them. But they, too, arc looking for peace and have little influence to make it happen," said Dagda.

"Sure, they do, they are the masses!" said Lynx.

"They need a light in the night, a guiding star. They are not pushing all the responsibility on you. They are the ones to rise to the occasion, liaising for hope. You have that advantage to do what they can not," said Dagda.

"And what is it that they can't do?" asked Lynx

"Kill Balor, of course, and lead in love and valour," answered Dagda.

"I don't think you will reason with your people in Balor. They have already died," said Dagda.

"But they survived. I just know it," answered Lynx.

"Balor is not the result of your people. Havoc echoes a greater whole of your people. No one should think they have this much power over the land where Balor is above morals. Led by residual ignorance of a time when he felt threatened, the need for structure and management is misguided in his way," said Dagda.

"People don't need hate to light their way. Fomorians survive in Balor; I can sense their presence," said Lynx.

"You will be fooled to death if you try to reason with and take power away from an insensible leader," said Dagda.

"You will not find your family in Balor when you face him. He is a stone-cold killer and will not think twice about absolving your life to move his power. Then he truly will be unstoppable; you are the key to their freedom, Lugh!" said Dagda.

"Don't say my name; he is close," said Lynx.

"You are wise beyond words and will persevere; do not fear who you are."

"Thanks for your confidence; I will try not to let you down."

"You will not disappoint me; I am proud of what you've become. I will be with you and not leave you again till we face Balor."

"Thanks, Dagda," said Lynx.

"Shall we make our way?"

A loud scratch from Halek echoes above their head. That's an attack call," said Dagda. "That hawk must have found lunch on the run."

"I don't think so, it's diving toward us," said Lynx.

The hawk flew closer. It was bigger than the average hawk, primarily black, with a wingspan twice the average size.

It was moving quickly and spreading its wings just before it hit the ground, landing on a large rock near Dagda and Lynx.

"What news do you have?" Dagda asked.

But the hawk just stared at them. Another voice spoke from behind the large rock.

"He is my eyes. We are both at your service," said a dark wolf as he walked out of the brush.

"I am Filtiarn. I was sent to watch Balor and bring news to you."

"What have you found?" asked Lynx.

"Balor is quickly moving; he has been south, likely looking for another passage into *Tig na nOg* from *Soilsiu Thiar*. It appears as if he is moving toward the Giant's gateway now. He will come to you if you stay here; he is walking along Lough Neagh," said Filtiarn.

"You are brave, Filtiarn; your allegiance in helping track him is appreciated," said Dagda.

"It's my honour; I will give my life to rid the underworld or all worlds in that matter of Balor's wrath. He has killed too many in the name of his way," said Filtiarn.

"I agree," said Lynx.

"Thanks for bringing the news. Dagda, we should slowly carry on south to meet him instead of waiting here," said Lynx.

"After you," Dagda said, touching Lynx on the shoulder. Dagda's heavy hand and warm smile shine through his thick beard. Lynx feels safe with Dagda, building confidence to overcome the challenge ahead.

"Balor may be so focused on his task that he will not expect us to confront him. Let's do this," said Dagda.

"If you walk south, Halek and I will accompany you. Halek's screech will give you a warning. If I can help, I'll be happy to. My fearlessness is yours," said Filtiarn, and he took flight.

Dagda had shown to be a great companion on the road. He was saving Lynx's life and remained a true friend. He always seemed to have an excellent approach to whatever situation he encountered; he never appeared to be under stress, despite his extensive knowledge. The circumstances would always maintain their grip on their present restraints and challenges.

"It's good that we have such great allies on our side. Balor does not know the fate we bring him," said Dagda.

"He may be very persuasive, pushing his threats on people. He doesn't foresee the fate we bring. Dagda, you certainly give me strength," said Lynx

Walking south for hours, laughing and telling old stories that brought about a more lighthearted time for Lynx. Soon they became inattentive to what lay ahead, a welcome break from the worry clouding his mind.

Ready for a break, they rested by a lake. Each settled into calming meditation, taking in the scenery of the dark, still lake. Lynx became mindful of the sound of silence to focus his senses on the force ahead of him.

A loud scratch from Halek broke the stillness, echoing through the rolling hills. Both looked up at each other.

"Trees!" Dagda said, getting up slowly but silently while walking into the woods, which was much louder. Compared to the loud steps approaching them, his noise did not seem to matter.

"What is that? I hear talking," said Lynx.

"No longer allowed to pass through the gate, how can they take this freedom from me? Finn will pay to trap me here when I gain access to *Tir na nOg*.

"Heaven will regret their overthrow."

Balor could be heard talking to himself in random nonsense.

Lynx gripped the spear entrusted to him.

"Easy," said Dagda.

"Three compasses and one land. Guide my hand; give it strength to bring light to the darkness, destroy that which poisons our island and kills my family."

He slowly steps out in front of Balor's path.

"Stay out of sight for now, Dagda; I must face him alone."

Lynx pulled up his hood to shadow his face and walked toward Balor. With his face hidden, he was standing in front of this much larger giant, passionate in his thoughts and trying not to get overly excited in his presence.

"What brings you down this way, Toraigh?"

"Why do you address me this way?" said Balor.

"Is this not who you are?"

"Don't test me, dark traveller, or I will turn you to stone. Long ago, my people called me Toraigh. That part of my life is long gone, and I'm much better off away from there," said Balor.

"That part of your life is who you will always be; you will never escape the unity. And it will be your downfall, your people against you," said Lynx.

"Is that so? Lying, Lugh!" said Balor.

"Your time is exhausted here, while mine is evolving; Now it's your turn to see the future. Your family waits; you will join them and rise to greatness," said Balor

"Nothing about you is great. I will see you die before I join you," Lynx said, gripping his spear.

"You're Fomorian; join me. Your strength is a raindrop against the ocean. We will welcome you."

"Or like a bullet to the brain," said Lynx.

"We could rule and govern this land together, my son."

"You are not my family. You are more like the village idiot. We were peaceful explorers who destroyed innocent people's lives and locked them up. You deserve no respect from me. Except when you look at the tip of my spear, you can appreciate the end of your miserable life," said Lynx.

"Such harsh words for someone trying to help you. If you don't join me, you will die," Balor said.

Lynx gripped his spear fast, got his arm back, launched it, and jumped up toward Balor's head, but as quick as Lynx was, Balor was faster, the spear just missing Balor's head as he dodged the lightning bolt coming at his head.

Lynx kept his momentum going with light energy, watching Balor dodge the spear. He reached out and pulled the spear back. As fast as he threw it, Lynx flew up at Balor as the spear returned. He caught the spear to jab at Balor's mask to get through the darkness of the iron mask he wore.

Balor off-guard; Lynx jabbed in hard at Balor's head. As he dodged again, Lynx landed a blow, breaking off part of the mask and exposing the light behind the mask a little more.

Balor laughed at Lynx as he landed back on the ground.

"Your strength and speed will never contrast with mine," Balor said, turning away and speeding north toward the Giant's gateway.

Dagda came out of the wood. "Coward didn't stick around very long. I'm sure you scared him with that blow to the mask. He's heading back to the Gateway. I fear the only way to survive the foretold demise at your hand is to get the spirit stone," said Dagda.

"Let's head back to the Gateway ourselves. He will be fast and desperate for survival, and the power of his manic rage will catch Finn unaware," said Lynx.

"Now he knows we are on his trail. Let's use light energy for transport," said Dagda.

They turned north and started running, disappearing as soon as they did and reappeared on the cliffs at the gateway.

The ground shook beneath their feet. A wave shot out from the shoreline.

Warning filled Dagda as his thoughts raced toward the worst at this moment. Lynx and Dagda approached the pillars to join Finn as he tried to predict Balor's moves. Finn pushed a post deep into the earth.

"So glad to see you, boys," Finn said with exhaustion.

Mr. Kitty ran out of the morning fog straight to where Dagda, Lynx, and Finn stood.

"What is happening?" asked Mr. Kitty.

"That's not an earthquake, Kitty," said Finn, driving another pillar deeper into the earth toward Balor.

"Let him come, Finn," said Lynx.

"Are you mad!" answered Dagda.

"He's coming; Finn has protected us for too long—the time has come," said Lynx

Mr. Kitty, very nervous, grabbed the stone Kara had given him. He ran to the shore, touching his tail to the water.

"Kara De Farraige. The time has come; Balor will soon push through the giant's gateway, and your help is needed," Mr. Kitty said.

Mr. Kitty was hit by an incoming wave, flying back and landing hard on the rocks.

Pillars flew out of the ground like a bomb had gone off. Pillars exploded in every direction, nearly hitting everyone.

Lynx ran closer to the hole that opened on the shore, gripping his spear, ready to welcome Balor back to *Tir na nOg*, with Dagda and Finn standing close behind.

Mr. Kitty lay unconscious on the rocks as the tide rose.

"Finally, you meet your end," a voice said from a large rock above Mr. Kitty's head.

Glic jumped out of the early morning darkness with his blade above his head to come down on Mr. Kitty, who was about to strike a blow.

Light surrounded Mr. Kitty as the light repelled Glic, pushing him with such force that it knocked the spirit stone out of his pocket.

Dair and Danu appear on the shore, but they are not quick enough to catch Glic. He grabbed the stone and the blade and quickly disappeared.

Dair picked up Mr. Kitty and moved away from the shore and Giant's gateway. From the underworld, Balor gathered light energy in his hands and threw large balls of energy at the giant pillars at his feet, exploding rock into the ground.

Giants came up over the cliffs in the underworld. They were running toward Balor.

"You have destroyed our land and peace too long, Balor of the evil way," a giant said.

Fifty giants stormed the hill. Enraged, Balor gathered madness at the sight of the giants' army.

"It's time to find your peace," Balor said as he fixed his gaze on the giants.

Balor's mask glowed with light, blinding the giants, and several turned to stone, encouraging Balor to explode into the ground. Pillars flew out on *Tir na nOg* as Balor pushed his giant self into the hole and out of the earth into *Tir na nOg*.

Chapter 18 Battle at the Gateway

Darkness blankets the misty sky;
The moon's fourth quarter is in line.
The foreshadowing of a lone crow's cry
and stillness stands the test of time.
Babd heeds the battle cry to mystify the enemy's mind.
A battle breaks, and strong will crumble, when the tower comes to
fall.
Songs of love shall dissolve the pain.
In heart and mind, like falling rain.
No energy shall raise the dead, find thy peace in the morning light
Souls will illuminate without fright.
All help is needed, and partnerships are required.
to cross the equinox and survive the season
Balor shall rise to an oath of treason,
but the power of love is beyond all reason.

Mr. Kitty was on the rocks of the Gateway, beaten down by the waves, giving Glic a chance to take his life. With the luck of the Irish, Dair was there to save him.

The ground rumbled beneath, and shock waves were evident in the water due to Balor's relentless determination to clear the Giant's gateway beneath Finn's feet.

"Kitty," Dair called. "Are you okay?"

"Please, I'm so sorry for bringing you into this mess. All you wanted to do was see fairies and leprechauns," Dair said.

"And merrows and stone circles," Mr. Kitty said in a low, shaken voice.

Dair picked Mr. Kitty up to embrace his new furry friend. "I must get you to safety," Dair said.

"I'm okay, just a little winded after hitting the rocks; I managed to call Kara and the merrows before getting thrown into the rocks," said Mr. Kitty

"There is no limit to the risk you put yourself in to save Ireland," said Danu.

"I just want to help what I can while I can," said Mr. Kitty.

"The world needs more like you, Kitty," said Danu.

Mr. Kitty's face brightened up when he addressed him this way.

"That is truly an honour coming from you, Danu. I hope I don't disappoint you," said Mr Kitty.

"You have already done more than expected," said Dair.

"We're not done yet. We should gather the circle and develop a plan. I don't know, but these earthquakes seem more intense," said Mr Kitty.

"We should join the others," said Dair.

"Finn, Dagda, and Lynx are not far up the shore, keeping Balor from busting through," said Mr. Kitty.

A massive explosion went off one hundred feet from the shore, hurling hexagonal stone pillars like pebbles out of the earth. When the water and stone returned to the sea, Mr. Kitty could see the ocean ripple with movement back toward the direction from which the explosion had come. Tips of tridents rush the area as the merrow warriors come to meet Balor—shoots of white light and tridents pebbled Balor from all angles.

Many initial tridents landed with great force, unable to find a weak spot in his armour. Climbing back into *Tir na nOg* from the water, dazed, he was trying to get his bearings. Another trident took another piece of his mask, making Balor even more vulnerable.

Enraged, Balor aimed with his evil eye, turning in quick circles, killing many marrows in his proximity. He gave a hard blow to hundreds as the merrows descended back to the depths. Balor walked up the beach, assessing the situation and aiming for the hills, but no one stood up, hidden in the shadows.

Finn, Dagda, and Lynx joined Mr. Kitty and the others on the other side of the stone gateway. Mr. Kitty saw movement and puffed up his tail. He sensed and smelled the shadow of Glic lurking and moved toward Balor.

"Glic! Now is my time!" Mr. Kitty said, letting out a hiss, before taking off.

The others looked at Mr. Kitty as he ran fast along the pillars like the wind.

"Kitty," Dair said out loud with no change in Mr. Kitty's focus.

"What is he doing?" asked Dair.

"Trust him," said Dagda.

"Keep an eye on him; he must have spotted the stone!" said Danu.

The shadow of Glic was stealthy, not enough for Mr. Kitty as he hit his head off and went into Glass's line to Balor.

Mr. Kitty had a good eye on Glic as he made his way. Creeping down close to the water, waiting for Glic to come his way, Kitty's tail touched the water, and no more than a minute later, Mr. Kitty heard an angelic voice.

"I am with you." Kara slowly emerged from the water.

"How did you find me?"

"You still have my necklace in your pocket; you are brave, Kitty," said Kara with a heartfelt smile.

"What is your plan here?" asked Kara.

"Glic has the spirit stone and is moving toward Balor; he is getting sloppy now, thinking no one is watching. I plan to intercept," said Mr. Kitty.

"Be safe," Kara said as Mr. Kitty jumped onto a stone pillar. Glic got closer, and then Mr. Kitty pounced down with claws hard enough to slash Glic's face from the left eye and down his cheek.

Mr. Kitty knocked Glic back to the rocks with his surprise attack. Mr. Kitty kept at him, hoping to dislodge the spirit stone from a pocket. He strategically attacked Glic to search his pockets while inflicting a few wounds, both for himself and to disable Glic from reaching Balor.

"Where is it?" asked Mr. Kitty.

"Where's what, you filthy feline?" snapped Glic.

"You know what!" Mr. Kitty held his claws to Glic's neck.

"Let's face it; you're too much of a pussycat to harm anyone," said Glic.

Mr. Kitty pushed his claw harder into Glics' neck till he punctured skin, and blood dripped.

"It's your choice, the stone or your death."

Balor saw the struggle on the rocks. Knowing Glic held the stone, he started to move toward them. Lynx, Dagda, and Dair also closely saw Balor moving in Kitty's direction, so they came out from the stone pillars to prevent any harm from coming to Mr. Kitty.

Merrows lined the shoreline with tridents in hand, firing them at Balor, making him look as Lynx got close enough to throw his spear like a lightning bolt, missing his head but instead going right through his armour into his shoulder.

He screamed in pain and desperation, pulling the spear from his shoulder. At the same time, tridents attacked him, bouncing off his armour.

Though short compared to Balor, Dagda was not affected by his light. Dagda managed to get close enough to swing his mighty club hard enough to hit Balor's knee from the side, taking Balor down.

Quickly lifting his club to come down at his head and landing a solid blow, sending him into a state of disorientation, Lynx pulled his spear back and came directly behind Dagda's blow. Balor managed to get his head to the side, barely missing Lynx's spear.

Giants were climbing out of the gateway that Balor opened. Balor aimed his evil eye, shooting light at the merrows on the shore while the giants marched their way. He turned to kick Dagda hard in the chest, taking his breath away as he flew back to the cliffs.

Merrows had blown to the shore from the impact, and some turned to stone. A few more giants turned to rock as they rushed out of the water to intercept his wrath.

Balor felt at a loss; many giants ran at him while he could not reach Glic, who was detained. Balor was hoping to free Glic as Mr. Kitty turned his back. Balor opened his eye in their direction, shocked enough to throw Mr. Kitty off Glic. Glic was also impacted, slamming him hard into the shoreline.

Balor was outnumbered and took off at the speed of light, and few could see which direction he went.

Stunned, Mr. Kitty could not get back to Glic quickly enough to get the stone or subdue him, and Glic followed Balor's exit.

Many merrows lay on the beach, injured, as the mass confusion began to settle.

Danu, Dagda, and Padraig quickly tended to the wounded.

"We must follow now!" said Lynx.

"Did anyone see which direction he went?" asked Mr. Kitty.

"He headed southeast and could be anywhere on the island at this point; he is strong and fast," said Lynx.

"I'm sorry, Sir Lynx, I did not get the stone from Glic," said Mr. Kitty.

"That was very brave, Kitty," said Lynx. "No one else would have the bravery to step between Balor and him, having the stone."

"I should have..." Mr. Kitty started.

"Don't!" said Dair. "You moved with stealth and prevented Glic from getting the stone to Balor. You are a hero."

"And you saved Ireland, for now, giving us time to track him," said Lynx.

"Glic got away and will know where Balor went," said Mr. Kitty.

"Balor may move fast, but Glic does not," said Dagda.

"We can track him," said Lynx.

"Glic is slippery; how will we find him?" asked Brigid.

"Not only is he a foul creature, but he also smells foul. His stink embeds in my senses," said Mr. Kitty.

"You surprise me over and over, Kitty," said Lynx.

Giants came to the beach with the spirit circle and brainstormed to develop a plan to follow Balor and Glic.

"Who will go with Kitty?" Asked Dagda.

Several spoke up, as all wanted to secure Mr. Kitty and save Glic from giving the stone to Balor.

"Not all can go. I recommend one or two to follow with Kitty," said Danu.

"Danu is right. We shouldn't attract too much attention. Otherwise, Glic will get suspicious and lead us in the wrong direction," spoke Lir.

"I will go," said Dair. "Kitty is my responsibility. I feel I should be near him."

"Very well," Danu said.

"I will also go; this is my destiny to face Balor," said Lynx.

"So be it," said Dagda.

"The three of you should hurry," said Danu.

"Lynx, my son. I'm not your real father, but I love you. Take this stone," said Lir.

Handing Lynx a translucent mauve and turquoise quartz stone, he said, "I have this stone's twin, and you can keep us in the know while not raising any of Balor's suspicions. Once you find him at the appropriate time, call the spirit circle, and we will be at your side quickly."

"You have been more than a father to me, and I love you just the same. My whole reason for being is because you were at the right place when Balor threw me into the unforgiving ocean," said Lynx.

"Dagda!" Padraig spoke. "Many merrows are injured and dying. Several giants are down, and my care is insufficient to save their lives; please help."

Dagda disappeared as quickly as a thought, and less than a minute later, he appeared back further down the beach, close to the bulk of the wounded, with his harp. A bulk of a man, rough and robust, tranquillity overcame the beach after the trauma they experienced.

Brigid, Danu, and Dagda cared for the injured on the beach, healing many wounds while calming those left behind by their lost comrades.

Mr. Kitty also drifted away, remembering his family and missing them dearly. He felt lost to them and sensed their pain of losing a loved one, even though he was not gone. Mr. Kitty wished he could see them now. I hope this is all a dream that he will wake up and hear Dally Dear's voice again, Wisdom the owl's kind words, or his brothers and sisters arguing.

With all the sorrow of being away from them, he felt connected to them through Dagda's music. The world now seemed so much smaller. All the worries he once had seemed so trivial.

"Come, Kitty," said Dair.

"Let's make our way to prevent Glic from getting too far ahead or even close to Balor. I will swiftly take you on a light stream unseen to Glic's senses," said Dair.

Mr. Kitty jumped up into Dair's arms. Lynx, Dair, and Mr Kitty disappeared as they turned south.

Chapter 19 Flee to Uisneach Hill

My home is my spirit, where my loved ones are bound.
Old bones will be worshipped and cared for through time.
Our memories are treasures; no gift is more sacred.
A dream settled in the hills of my heart.
Working hard to ease the pain of our family's old age.
Forced pace to make a change, the fall season breaks will be.
My home is my strength; bring all tenderness in.
Our circle is growing; the love light burns bright,
Open up my devotion; efforts strengthen the fight.
One life to share our love to build a most pleasant shelter.
Many lives have been saved in the land of the present.
My home is my Spirit.

"I'm a child of Earth; time can't hold its restraints on me. I must open the door, not for me but for those who follow and my loved ones to find me. The scent grows stronger, foul like a poison that will choke me." Mr. Kitty's thoughts raced as he cut through matter on Dair's shoulder, accompanied by Lynx. They were tracking Glic as he made his way closer to Balor.

"Kitty, are you with us?" asked Dair.

"I'm here. The stink grows stronger. I believe we are near, as my fear also seems to grow in Glic's presence," said Mr. Kitty.

"Fear is our beacon in the night; when you are unsure what the truth is, trust your gut to guide you," said Lynx. "Fear is not a weakness but a strength as long as you know how to use it."

"I will need all the help I can get," said Mr. Kitty.

"We are here with you; you will never be alone, Kitty," said Lynx.

"My gut tells me I must face Glic alone to get the stone. Maybe you can take me ahead of him, and once he gets closer to Balor, I can talk face-to-face with Glic."

"I see Balor," said Lynx. "He is at the centre of the island."

"We should take cover then; Glic is moving fast," said Dair.

"We are past him; I lost his scent," said Mr. Kitty.

"So be it," said Lynx.

The three landed not far from Balor, just outside Uisneach Hill.

"We part here; it's time for stealth mode," said Mr. Kitty. "I should watch for Glic here."

"We will be close, Kitty. Just call us if you need assistance," said Dair.

"I should do my interception too," said Lynx, gripping his spear.

"Once you get the stone, we must take it to Lynx to destroy Balor. Call me, and I will assist you with getting away," said Dair.

"Thanks, Dair. Good luck, Lynx," Mr. Kitty said as he silently disappeared into the bushes.

Mr. Kitty's desire to save Ireland from Balor and the fear he drummed up for himself in this predicament were contradictory forces in his heart. Fearing facing Glic again, having nearly died twice already, he hoped his luck hadn't run out.

"You can do this," he said to himself, taking a deep breath and crouching down, slipping into the tuft of trees to wait for Glic.

"What have I gotten into? How can I follow through with this? I can't get out of it now. I could leave, but I would never. Getting the stone is the right thing, as difficult as it is," Mr. Kitty thought as his mind jumped around with anxiety, trying to understand his purpose here.

"If I leave, I will live to die another day, and I will have failed myself. Everybody is so lovely here; if I can help, I should. I am fortunate to help," Mr. Kitty thought.

Mr. Kitty heard rustling through the brush.

"I picked the right spot to watch for Glic," he thought.

Mr. Kitty climbed to a branch in a tree to watch for Glic as Glic made his way to the edge of the brush. He paused to peek back at the open field for any sign of the spirit circle or even to see Balor himself.

Mr. Kitty remained still, away from Glic's line of vision.

"We have to stop meeting like this," Mr. Kitty said; Glic hissed. Wild fright overcame him as he jumped back.

"Who's there? Show yourself."

"I told you, you will die if you don't give up the stone," said Mr. Kitty.

"It's under new management now, fat cat. Either you bow to me directly or serve me later," said Glic.

Mr. Kitty dropped out of the tree, catching Glic by surprise. He dug his claw deep into Glic's eye, missing his other eye. He slashed his neck with his hind claws. Glic reacted quickly, flinging Mr. Kitty from his head.

"My eye, you filthy shoe brush."

Mr. Kitty jumped back quickly at Glic, holding his neck and pointing his claw at his other eye.

"The stone!" Mr. Kitty said sternly.

"You can take the stone from me, but you will not escape Balor. He is just over the hill. He will sense me by now," said Glic.

"I have more angles of support to escape Balor. He can't harm me if I realize he does not affect me," said Mr. Kitty.

"Fool, Balor is unstoppable now!" Glic said, spitting blood at Mr. Kitty.

"The stone," Mr. Kitty said, digging his claws further into Glic's skin.

Glic reached into his pocket, pulled out the stone, and handed it to Mr. Kitty. He grabbed the stone, but removing his claws from Glic's neck allowed him to catch his little blade and swing it at Mr. Kitty, cutting his shoulder, causing Mr.Kitty to fall off.

Mr. Kitty got up quickly, fleeing toward Uisneach Hill into the open as Glic chased him. Not having his stealthy skills when he could not hide, Glic caught up with Mr. Kitty, jumping on his back.

Tucking his head, he rolled to his back, knocking Glic off. Mr. Kitty knocked the knife out of Glic's hand. Both jumped at the knife, and Mr. Kitty managed to grab it. Mr. Kitty was polydactyl, with an extra toe like a thumb gripping the handle. With one motion of jumping at Glic, the stone flew out of his pouch.

Mr. Kitty saw the stone, reached out to save it, and wrestled with Glic; Glic was much stronger than Kitty and turned the knife at him.

The knife slipped into Mr. Kitty's chest. He had never felt a sting like this, shocks of pain that sent needles through his system. He fell to the ground, feeling a loss of energy. With his head dizzy, he looked over to see the spirit stone.

Light shifted as Dair took form in front of him. Dair then shot a force at Glic, sending him ten feet from Mr. Kitty.

"No! Kitty," Dair said, dropping to his knees.

Mr. Kitty was barely conscious as he bled. "This is where we part, Dair."

"No, Kitty."

"The stone," Mr. Kitty said, holding out his paw.

"Stop the madness now, Balor," said Lynx.

"It's not for you to say; it's beyond you now. I'm too strong and hold all the power," said Balor.

"No one holds all the power; you're delusional," said Lynx.

"You don't know anything, young Lugh," Balor replied.

"I'm not so young anymore, Balor. It's time for peace. I'm here to change this fear you conjured," said Lynx.

He gripped his spear, which had been in his family for thousands of years, having been passed down to him from his mother. Lynx's spear started to sense the stone over the hill, as Mr. Kitty gave his life to his energy.

Balor towers over Lynx. From his head to the soles of his feet, the dark iron armour he wears acts to protect him and cage the light of his captives.

Balor also feels the stone as his desire for power turns to rage. In his conspiracy-driven mind, he believes he will not die if he holds the spirit stone. He turns toward Mr. Kitty and Dair, drawing on the stone and wanting to take control.

Lynx quickly sped ahead of Balor, seeing him turn. Quickly getting to Dair and finding Mr. Kitty not moving on the ground, he knelt on one knee to see the knife in his chest.

"What happened?" Lynx asked, reaching down to pet Mr. Kitty, feeling empathy for the loss of a kind, gentle spirit.

"Glic has stabbed him," said Dair, knowing the blood loss is too much, and Mr. Kitty is critical.

"Sad to say, we are all about to die. Balor is towering over us, as you see. We need to get out of here," Lynx said.

"Kittys is too ill to travel anywhere. We need Dagda," said Dair.

"Kitty rescued the stone!" Dair said, handing it to Lynx.

Lynx took the stone, holding the spear in his other hand. He noticed the stone fit under the blade's arrowhead and pushed it in place.

Balor looked down at Lynx, Dair, and Mr. Kitty.

"You're the one who wants peace," Balor said as he reached out to take the stone from Lynx.

"You're not about peace; you bring destruction while thinking everyone is standing in your way. A true leader would fix problems, not create misery for everything in its path." Lynx said.

"You will see the power of the light," Balor said as he threw his sword at Lynx and ran at him.

Lynx quickly diverted the blade, but Balor's momentum kept him moving forward long enough for Lynx to drive his spear through Balor's mask of light.

Balor began to shine brightly with the light emanating from his head. A tower of iron, flooding the sky with a beacon of light, turned into a dark, misty smoke cloud. His suit of armour dropped to its knees, and Lynx pulled the spear out of the dark volcanic ash that remained.

Balor's light turned to dark mist, which formed into thousands of crows that circled Lynx, Dair, and Mr. Kitty.

A large raven landed in front of them and took the form of Lynx's mother, Enyu.

"Lynx, Kitty is dead; the stone must save him," said Dair.

Lynx looked at his mother as he removed the stone from the spear. Without saying a word, she took the stone and placed it on his chest, turning him to stone.

"It has killed Kitty!" Looking at his mother, he was concerned. "What have you done?"

"No one could save Mr. Kitty from his path. This was the most appropriate way to honour his life. He gave his life for the sake of the stone.

Balor was in control of us, captive in his delusions. We lived in all three worlds as crows, unable to affect Balor's decisions in *Tir na nOg*. We were unable to do anything about what we knew, given our knowledge of the past, present, and future. But you set us free," Enyu said.

"Where is Balor?" asked Lynx.

"You killed him. He is the shell left behind in the ash," said Enyu.

"If you knew the spirit stone would turn Kitty into a cat stone, why would you place it on him?" said Lynx.

"He passed away before we placed the stone on his chest. No one can bring a mortal back to life. Mr. Kitty has sacrificed his life for the sake of the stone and the island's freedom.

Allowing him to be the spirit stone connecting all three worlds in time was appropriate. You three are the key. Now, this is the thinnest place on earth. A symbol of peace, light and unity," said Enyu.

Dagda showed up with the rest of the spirit circle. Saddened by the news that Mr. Kitty had passed, they surrounded Mr. Kitty's stone.

After a short silence, Mr. Kitty took form on top of the cat-stone.

"What?" said Dair. "How?"

"Mr. Kitty is born to *Tir na nOg* from the other world," said Enyu.

In amazement, they all stared at Mr. Kitty, having been here to experience the death of a mortal born to *Tir Na nOg*.

"Mr. Kitty, welcome back to *Tir na nOg*," said Dair.

Mr. Kitty slowly raised his chin, feeling only love and light connected to his family and those surrounding him.

"I shall not return to my former life, shall I?" Mr. Kitty asked.

"No!" said Dagda. "You have been awakened. There is no going back to who you once were. You are now over the rainbow bridge."

Glossary

Bru - Hospice or the centre of Newgrange; A bridge to nowhere.

Ceo - mist

Dia dhuit - (jee-ah gwit) God bless you

Dia Maith - (jee-ah M'ah) Good God, refers to Dagda

Equinox- Time when day and night are equal in length; March 20 and September 23

Mhor bais - (vor buys) Big Death

Ta dinnear a seirbheail- (Din-yare a shar-a-val) Dinner is served

Tir na nOg - (Tier na nohg) Realm of the youth, where multi-dimensional beings reside.

Soilsiu Thiar - (Sail su hier) Illuminate west; Newgrange.

Solstice - Longest day of the year, June 21; Shortest day of the year, December 21

Characters

Mr. Kitty- Kit Cat or Kitty

Aedan - Woodland Fairy

Alta - General of Owl Parliament, resides near Randalstown

Aos Si or (eess see)- Supernatural, fairy ancestors, take form individual to the seer.

Athair - Woodland Fairy King - Hazel's Father

Badb- Celtic goddess, The Morrigan. Takes the form of a Crow to warn of battle

Balor- Fomorian from Rathlin Island, migrated to Ireland with some of his Kin.

Brigid- Druid Goddess, acquired prophecy and divination, Daughter of Dagda

Caoranach- Finn's enemy, banished to Lough Derg

Clio- (Kleeo) Little girl in the park. Kleena is having a dream.

Dagda or Eagna, the God of Life and Death, built Newgrange

Dair -Druid, Mr. Kitty's guide, Spirit of the oak

Danu or Anu- The most ancient goddess, Tuatha de Danann

Enyu (Ethniu)- Lynx Mother

Femi- Falcon Pooka

Filtiarn- Wolf Pooka

Finn McCool -Built the Giant's Gateway, and in this story, is Dagda's son.

Fomorian - A sea-dwelling supernatural race that landed in Ireland for refuge but brought war when they found unacceptance and resistance

George - Short, stout pirate troll at Grange stone circle

Glic - Dark Elf

Hazel - Woodland Fairy Princess, daughter of Athair

Halek- Hawk Pooka

Kara De Farraige - Merrow or mermaid. Princess daughter of Ri

Kleena -(Cliodhna), Banshee and Spirit of the Known: Heals the sick with song and is accompanied by three spirits that usually take the form of birds

Luminous beings- Light spirits of the Known

Lynx - Lugh- Balor's grandson, last of the Formorians, master of skills and light

Man Mac Lir - God of Sea and Isle of Man. From the afterlife. Saved Lynx from drowning and raised him. Tuatha De Danann

O'Daimhin - Divine Ox of Knowth, the spirit of knowledge

Padraig or Maewyn or St. Patrick, Patron Apostle of Ireland

Pooka -Mischievous shapeshifter of *Tir na nOg*, horse, rabbit, raven, wolf, dog, or goblin

Ri De Farraige- King of the Merrow

Richard Og De Burg - Master of the house, Dunluce Castle

Runda - Leprechaun

Samwin - Divine Mother goddess, Spirit of Earth and fire, lives at the Core.

Saoi (see) - the Divine Ox or O'Daimhin

Shannon - Patron of Ireland

Sinsear - Pooka Elder

Three Sisters

> **Banba**, the Goddess of Ireland, is said to be her final resting place at the Ballynoe stone circle.

> **Eriu** - Goddess of Ireland's Sovereignty, Uisneach is her final resting place.

> **Fodla**- Power of the land, Drombeg stone circle is her final resting place

Toraigh (Tory)- Early name of Balor. He had a fort on Tory Island during his seafaring

Tuatha De Danann- A Supernatural race of Ireland; the Tribe of God

Places

Ballynoe stone circle- Megalithic stone circle in Northern Ireland.

Cat Stone- Located at Hill of Uisneach. Stone of divisions, and burial of Goddess Eriu

Cliffs of Mohr - Southwest on the island. Towering one hundred and twenty metres out of the ocean. Stories of otherworldly beings run deep in these hills.

Dunluce Castle- A Medieval castle in Northern Ireland, located on the ocean cliffs of Basalt. Not far from the Giants' Gateway

Dromberg stone circle- South on the Island near Glandore in the County of Cork

Giant's Gateway- A natural, mysterious hexagonal basalt stone formation in Northern Ireland known as the Giant's Causeway

Grange Stone Circle, located in the County of Limerick, is the largest circle built over four thousand years ago.

Knowth- Prehistoric monument on the River Boyne, Part of the Bru trio with Newgrange and Dowth

Newgrange- A Bru stone monument built by Dagda. Over five thousand years old. On the winter solstice, the jewel in the east lights the path in winter, peace be to the eye.

Randalstown- North of Lough Neagh, home of Alta and woodland Fairies

Rathlin - an Island off the coast of Northern Ireland, Balor's home where he grew up

Tory Island- North-west coast of Ireland, Balor established a settlement there with his crew, pillaged and displaced many settlers, before bringing his havoc to Ireland.

Lough Na Suil- Lake of the Eye, a battle where Balor and Lynx fight over the spirit stone. This released energy wave causes the lake to disappear occasionally.

Loch Deary - Caoranch, Finn's rival, is banished too

Lough Neagh is the Largest lake in Ireland and a magical wonder of the spirit world

Uisneach Hill - Sacred centre of the Island, home of the cat stone, where many divisions begin and end

Tim Cross is from Cape Breton. He started a journey to help people, so he became a Registered Nurse. After years in critical care, he now works in palliative and end-of-life care. He moved from Nova Scotia to Alberta, where he met his loving wife, and they had a healthy girl. Writing is his opportunity to put both fears and hopes on paper, helping him navigate emotions and thoughts, and find peace in imagination. *Tir na nOg* is a point of interest that continues to fascinate his imagination. Ireland will always be his Honeymoon.

Embark on a journey into the characters of Irish Folklore with Mr. Kitty, a precarious, enlightened cat. Diving into 5000 years of Irish tales, as he travels across Ireland in the spirit realm of *Tir na nOg*, an alternate dimension alongside our own.

Tim Cross